Lost in Liberia

The Travel Blogger and the Fixer
(A Mama's Travel Agency Novel)

A novella

Desert Sands Publishing

Lost in Liberia is a work of fiction. Names, characters, places and incidents are products of the author's imagination or are used fictitiously and are not to be construed as real. Any resemblance to actual events, locales, organizations, or persons, living or dead, is entirely coincidental.

Published by
DESERT SANDS PUBLISHING
PO. Box 6556
Lancaster, CA 93539

Copyright © 2023 by Kimberly Sandhu
Cover: QDesign, www.qcoverdesign.com

ISBN-13: 978-1-7345692-8-5 (ebook)
ISBN-13: 978-1-7345692-9-2 (paperback)

All rights reserved. No part of this book may be reproduced or transmitted in any form or by any electronic or mechanical means, including photocopying, recording or by any information storage and retrieval system, without written permission of the publisher, except where permitted by law. For information address Desert Sands Publishing.

First Desert Sands Publishing: August 2023
10 9 8 7 6 5 4 3 2 1

If you purchased this book without a cover you should be aware that this book is stolen property. It was reported as "unsold and destroyed" to the publisher and neither the author nor the publisher has received any payment for this "stripped book."

ACKNOWLEDGMENTS

To my writing posse, A.M Roark and Leigh Adams, thanks for all of your time, love, and support.

Lost in Liberia

The Travel blogger and the Fixer
(A Mama's Travel Agency Novel)

Chapter 1

Mama's Travel Agency
Somewhere near Foggy Bottom metro station,
Washington DC

*T*anzy

Have you ever heard the old saw about life, lemons, and lemonade? Yeah, that one. When life throws you lemons, turn 'em into lemonade. If I hear it one more time, I'm gonna snatch my wig off and go running straight into the hills. All right, maybe nothing so dramatic. I'll keep my wig on, a girl's gotta look cute at all times, but I'd run off somewhere screaming.

Just left my job this afternoon. Or rather, my job left me. Fifth one in six months and that's a record. Strange stuff always happens around me, then I get blamed and ultimately fired. This time was not my fault, really it wasn't. I was hired as an IT specialist. Took the training and everything. The job was going smoothly until I saw a strange line of code and fixed it. My 'fix' was not the reason the entire building blacked out in the middle of the day. Try telling that to my boss though. They threw me out, once the elevators started to work again and they rescued about thirty people.

Anyway, I promised myself if this job went south, I'd become an entrepreneur. Hire my own damn self and start working at what I want to do, travel the world, see exotic stuff, do something fun and blog about it. It's called travel blogging. I'm free now and all in for the adventure.

I decided to head straight to my grandmother's travel agency. It wasn't far, just two exits on the metro. It was a typical DC day, the crowd pushed past me as I left the train. We flowed toward the exit machine; my feet carried me to the farthest one on the right. It usually worked for me, unlike the other three. A flip of the wrist to wave the travel card over the sensor and I would be on my way. The sensor flashed red, but the orange barrier didn't slide aside to let me pass. A quick glance over to the other three devices showed they worked just fine, passenger after passenger whipped by me. The gate opened for them like the parting of the Red Sea.

"You see, this is the kinda shit I don't need today, of all days," I said to a raven-haired hipster whose nose and lips sported impressive metal studs. She shrugged her shoulders, stepped around me, waved her card over the sensor, and passed on through.

I tried the next exit and then the next, but still no dice. I was on the third when a kind attendant dressed in a well-worn uniform stepped to my aid. A mop of gray coils fringed his shiny pate. He sort of reminded me of my Uncle Fred, except this guy carried a few more pounds around his middle.

"Can I help you, miss?"

I waved my card over the sensor with the same results as the other three. "Why is it I can't get out of the metro without some sort of card drama? I mean look, it won't work. This always happens to me," I grumbled.

He held his hand out. "Let me see," he said with a small grin creasing his lips. He passed the card over the sensor, a green light flashed on the screen, and voila, freedom. I stepped through and the barrier snapped closed, barely missing my rear.

"Here, miss, don't forget your card," he said with a toothy grin.

I reached back and snagged the card from his grasp like it was an offending appendage. I had no business being mad at the guy, he did just release me from metro purgatory. It was his smug look that grated on my nerves. Not everyone has this much bad luck with these devices. I swear there was a gremlin inside of the gate, eagerly rubbing his hands in anticipation of my arrival. Then when I show up, he presses a red button marked Tanzy and the whole system goes bonkers right in front of my eyes. Jeez.

I took a deep, calming breath and made a beeline for the exit, grateful for the fresh air and blue sky above. Outside, the street was crowded with tourists, the spring DC sun beat down from above. A cooling breeze blew in fitful puffs. Several blocks down on the right a brightly colored door appeared. The window, decorated with stencils, advertised the name:

LOST IN LIBERIA

Mama's Travel Agency
Call us if ya just gotta go!

Inside a waft of cool, refrigerated air greeted me. The scent of oranges mixed with cinnamon and spices filled the air. A couple of ladies sat at a small table full of colorful brochures. The walls were emblazoned with stencils of a beach full of palm trees with a glowing orange sunset dipping below the horizon. It felt like walking into a Caribbean dream, complemented by the low, muted tones of soca music playing in the background. At the far end of the room, my grandmother, Mama J, leaned over the shoulder of one of her employees. I didn't recognize the young lady and assumed she must've been new to the agency.

"Come on over, Tanzy darling," she said with a wave. "We've been waiting for you." Mama J wore her patent bright orange outfit. Today it came in the form of a jumpsuit with a red belt and bright red necklace. Her hair was carefully coiled atop her head in a swirl of gray glory.

I paused to look at the new display she erected on a side counter. A miniature Ferris wheel rotated in front of a photo of a beachfront pier full of amusement park themed entertainment. Each arm had a little gondola with a luggage fob bedecked with rhinestones attached to them. The travel agency logo was embossed on the back. I tend to have sticky fingers where sparkly stuff is concerned, so I plucked one from the wheel and continued on over to speak to Mama J.

"These fobs are a nice touch, Ma."

"I know, my logo designer just delivered them yesterday. Couldn't wait to put them out on display. That being said, you sounded excited when you called me. What's up?"

"First, thanks for seeing me on such short notice."

"You know I'm always here for you. I want you to meet Niecy, my new assistant."

"Hiya," she said with a wave.

"Well, I've decided to get started on my travel blog and needed help booking my reservations."

"A travel blog?" Mama J raised an eyebrow. "What about that new job of yours?"

"It wasn't for me," I evaded the question.

"Oh, Lord. What happened this time?"

"Nothing, and it wasn't my fault," I said too quickly.

"You lost another job?" She lowered her eyes and shook her head.

She said it in a defeated tone like she was halfway hopeful I'd make a month but came up a few weeks short. I'm ever the optimist if only to maintain my sanity. Besides, a positive attitude goes a long way. "You make it sound like a bad thing. This just means I get to strike out on my own and start fresh."

"And where is fresh going to take you?" she said with a sigh.

"I was thinking Liberia."

"I'm not sure Liberia is ready for you," she said.

LOST IN LIBERIA

"I'll be just fine. Nothing could go wrong. I'll have my own timetable and itinerary."

A tall, handsome sip of water stepped through the back door that led from the inner offices. He walked with a cool confident air as if nothing or no one could knock him off his game. He was slender, his gait light, his smile warm. The suit he wore was tailored and fitted. The jacket barely concealed the muscular six-pack he sported underneath. Drool leaked out of my gaping mouth before I could catch it. I immediately pressed my lips closed and plastered a sweet smile on my face. He stepped by me without a second glance.

"Are my documents ready?" he asked Mama J. Even his voice gave me goosebumps. It was a smooth baritone that I could listen to all day. He clasped a Styrofoam cup in his right hand. Steam curled from the top, delivering the smell of strong coffee with a hint of chicory.

"I almost have this program figured out. I'll be able to set up your online itinerary in a jiff," Niecy said. She reached over the desk and retrieved a white envelope. It bulged in the middle but otherwise had no markings. Mama J took it from her and opened it up.

"Okay, Phil, here's your package." She pulled a folded piece of paper from the envelope along with one of her new Ferris wheel fobs. It sparkled from the sunlight streaming in through the window.

"It's a bit flashy, don't you think?" Phil drawled.

"It'll be fine. We were under the gun to get it done before you arrived. Now, be sure to attach it to your carry-on bag."

"Yes, ma'am," he said.

Mama J slipped the items back into the envelope and handed it to Phil. My grandmother was smooth, I'll give her that. She made everything that happened in her travel agency look like a daily routine. To the outer world, Phil was picking up his travel documents and a luggage tag as a parting gift. The paperwork was probably his instructions, and the fob probably had a memory device or something in it. They could not fool me, but I knew the game, kept my face neutral, and played along.

Normally, in these situations, I would remain in the background. Things tend to go awry when I get excited, plus Mama J begged me to stay clear of the people from her back office. This fine specimen was clearly one of Mama J's agents. I applied once to work for the spy organization that she operates and was immediately told no. I would've made a great spy if they gave me a chance. Anyway, I honored her request and steered clear of all her *special* clients. Except, today was a new day and I was a new Tanzy.

"Hi, I'm Tanzy, and you are?"

"Oh, this is Phil. Phil, meet Tanzy," Mama J offered.

"Pleased to meet you," he said with a nod.

I moved to shake his free hand faster than fast and connected with the cup of steaming joe on the way. The cup toppled from his hand, turning end over end toward the floor. Hot liquid splashed on Phil and Mama J, leaving a trail of droplets in its wake. The coffee also landed on Niecy's keyboard. She jumped and rolled back into Phil, giving his leg a good thwack. The envelope slipped from his hands and in a graceful arc, landed smack-dab in the middle of the growing puddle of hot coffee. The contents tumbled out onto the floor. I reached to steady Mama J and lost the grip on my fob. It joined Phil's envelope and fob on the floor. I successfully managed to right my grandmother with Phil's help but she was already in a snit and clearly working up to a rage.

"Tanzy!" Mama J yelled.

Phil released Mama J and rubbed his shin. Niecy's chair made a nice imprint on his pant leg.

"I'm so sorry." I tried to pat away the growing stain on Phil's suit then Mama J's. "Are you okay? It didn't burn you, did it?"

"I'll survive," Phil said all the while brushing the front of his now stained suit. His eye twitched for a second. "Are you okay?"

"I got a little on my hand. It stung like the dickens but otherwise, I'm good. It's just that messes seem to follow me," I said in apology.

"I was speaking to Mama J." Phil was annoyed for sure.

"I'm fine," she grated from between clenched teeth.

Niecy ran to the bathroom, returned with a towel, and pushed it into my hand. "Here, this should help with the cleanup."

She ushered Mama J to the back of the agency where a door led to her private office. A string of epithets followed in their wake.

"Niecy, I'm all right," she yelled as Niecy fussed

over her.

"Yeah, but isn't she the one you said is a walking disaster waiting to happen?"

The door closed and their conversation became muffled.

"I'm so sorry about your suit."

"No worries." He flashed me a toothy smile that stole my heart. He bent to retrieve the envelope and its contents. "Looks like you dropped your fob as well." He picked mine up and handed it to me before scooping his dripping items.

"Your paper is soaked. Maybe they can print you a new page and I'll go grab a dry fob from the display."

"Don't worry, I'll manage. I'll dry everything out at the hotel." I handed him the towel Niecy gave me and he wrapped the items, moisture quickly seeping through.

"Hotel? Are you visiting?" The question slipped from my mouth before I could stop.

"I'm here for a short stay. Then I leave for Liberia."

"Me too. I've always wanted to visit Africa and decided to start there. Maybe we'll see each other."

He raised an eyebrow. "Oh, I doubt it. I'm not going to Africa."

"But you said…"

"Hey, I'm back," Niecy interrupted. The keyboard and desk were quickly cleaned and set to rights. She even had a replacement cup in her hand, this time a lid covered the top. "Here you go, Phil. Mama J said to give you these instructions and send you on your way."

LOST IN LIBERIA

She handed him a dry envelope, readjusted her seat, and sat down in front of her terminal.

"It was nice meeting you," Phil said. He flashed a dimpled smile, exposing a row of pearly whites, shook my hand, and was out the door in the blink of an eye.

"Now, about your trip," Niecy began. "You're going to Liberia?"

"Uhm, yes," I answered, still preoccupied with Phil's smile. "Just like Phil."

"Okay. How soon do you want to travel?"

"Tomorrow will be fine," I answered absently. There was nothing keeping me here and I didn't want to hear a thing from my mother or Mama J, for that matter, about the loss of yet another job. I had my passport in hand and only needed to pack a few essentials. This was going to be a three-day trip, so I planned to travel light.

She typed for a few seconds. "I have a flight leaving for Liberia Airport out of Dulles tomorrow at ten AM. I believe you're in luck. It's a nonstop. Do you want me to add on hotel reservations? Any preferences?"

"Just give me a nice place to stay. He is good-looking though."

"Who?"

"Tall dark and Phil," I answered.

"He's not for you. He's been having a hard time lately." Niecy finished typing and sent the information to the printer. I imagined running into him on my trip. He had such kissable lips and dreamy bedroom eyes. I could not imagine someone as fine as him having any trouble at all. "What? Unlucky at love and finding water?" I joked.

10

"Something like that. He refuses to date, and is married to his job." She pulled my itinerary from the printer. "Okay, here you go. You're all set."

"Thanks." I took the documents without a glance and headed out the door, spinning my shiny new glammed-out luggage fob around my index finger. Tomorrow was a new day and with each new day came a fresh start. At least that's what I always told myself because if I started every day with a disaster, I'd never get out of bed.

Chapter 2
Early the next morning

*P*_{hil}

"**W**hat do you mean it's not working?"

I pressed the button on the luggage fob a second and then a third time. Mama J was on the other end of the line, I had her on speaker. It was time to sync up with their computer at the agency and the damned thing would not start.

"We are getting nothing on our end. Try it again."

The frustration was clear in her voice. I tapped the button one last time. "Check it now. Do you have anything at all?"

"No, nothing. Flip it over and find a small depression in the middle of my logo. You'll have to do a hard reset."

Life as a spy was not all glamor and glitz. It could be somewhat boring. The last few assignments have all been the same. A quick flight into a country, do the assignment—usually a quick repair job—then a flight home. Pretty straightforward spy stuff. This trip was a little unusual as I was going to drop off a piece of tech for a minor operation down in Costa Rica. The mission depended on me syncing up the signal here with the fob I picked up yesterday. A chip was embedded inside…or so I thought.

The success of an assignment hinged on the preparation before you start. Always press, test, and go was my motto. I checked the logo on the reverse side. An image of an African woman embossed over a heart gleamed in the lamplight. There were no dimples and nothing to press.

"I don't see a spot to push. You sure you gave me the right one?"

There was dead silence on the other end of the phone. No one ever questioned Mama J, that was cardinal rule number one. I'd just stepped over the line. This trip had gone from bad to worse and I hadn't left the room.

"What did you just say?" she whispered. Uh-oh, she gave me the whisper. This was her quiet-before-the-storm voice. My blood ran cold but I held my ground. The mission depended on everything being tight and right. A little recap of yesterday's event seemed to be in order.

"Mama J, you processed the request from our agent in Central America, arranged for my flight to Liberia, had me come in when the fob was prepped and ready, introduced me to Tanzy, handed me the envelope, and I left." The twitch over my left eye kicked in. I ignored it and concentrated on keeping my voice level. If this was going to be a fight, I'd rather have it now than in the field where my options would be limited.

LOST IN LIBERIA

She hissed. "Repeat that last part." Her voice returned to normal. Now I was really confused. Not only was she not whispering, she sounded haunted. Like the world would collapse. "I took the envelope and left."

"Noooo, the part before that," she yelled.

"You introduced me to Tanzy." I had trouble understanding what she had to do with this conversation. The young lady was cute and funny. She was a bit clumsy and bumped into my cup of coffee, but accidents do happen. If I had time, I would have invited her out to dinner. But such was my life, I'm good at what I do and in high demand. Personal time always took a back seat to my job. I had a laundry list of failed relationships to prove it.

"Tanzy! No, not Tanzy. Why me, Lord? Why me?" The rest was incoherent. I heard Niecy in the background describing the mess on the floor and how she replaced my cup of coffee and paperwork.

"Mama J. What's going on?"

"Phil, I will say this once. Tanzy James is a walking disaster. If shit can go wrong, it will go wrong where she's concerned. Bad luck flows off her like stink off a dung beetle." Her voice cracked with emotion, as if she were resigned to a fate she wanted to avoid, yet one the gods had preordained.

"That's a bit harsh." I didn't want to contradict her but damn it, Tanzy seemed like a nice lady. "Don't you think you're overreacting?"

"Overreacting?" She was yelling again. "Let me guess, she had a fob in her hand too. It landed on the floor next to yours in the collision. Ever the gentleman, you picked everything up and handed it back to her. Phillip, you gave her your fob by mistake. Don't you see? This kind of thing happens on the regular whenever Tanzy is around. My God, I had to ban her from the bathrooms here at the office. Do you know how many times I called a plumber because she flushed and it overflowed? You can't run a business this way." She stopped, clearly out of breath.

As for me, I was in shock. The Mama J I knew never went on a tirade for situations like this. It was like Tanzy triggered her in some way. But the other more worrying aspect of her statement was the part about the fobs.

"I gave her mine and took hers?" My right eye twitched a samba to match my racing heart, a physical reaction to situations beyond my control. Most times I was able to control it. Then there were other times the muscles moved back and forth of their own volition. Case in point, this assignment was heading south and I'd not left the room. There was going to be a slight detour and my target was heading in the opposite direction. "She said she was booking a flight to Africa leaving today."

I inhaled a calming breath and rubbed the heel of my palm into the spot above my eye. Had to slow it down so I could think straight. *Where was that strong coffee when you needed it?* "What time is her flight? Maybe I can intercept her before she leaves. I won't have time to fly to Africa and double back to Costa Rica."

LOST IN LIBERIA

Niecy and Mama J spoke in hushed tones for a couple of minutes before I got an answer. "Phil, we may have caught a break," Mama J started. "Tanzy did come here looking for a ticket to the country of Liberia in Africa."

"Yes, that's what I'd guessed."

"But the Tanzy effect kicked in." Mama J actually chuckled.

I was not sure I liked the sound of her laugh, but it seemed that anything concerning Tanzy was enough to throw Mama J off her game.

"Oh, please do explain." I was at a complete loss at this point and could not imagine how things could get any weirder.

"It seems in all of the mix-up yesterday, Tanzy, being Tanzy, didn't understand that you were heading to the city of Liberia in Costa Rica instead of the country of Liberia in Africa. She asked Niecy to make her ticket like yours." She stifled a snort. "And Niecy, not aware she wanted the country instead of the city, booked her a flight to Liberia, Costa Rica. She leaves at ten this morning."

"Surely to goodness, she's going to notice she's heading to the wrong city on the wrong continent in the wrong hemisphere!" I wanted to give Tanzy the benefit of the doubt. There was no way she was as bad as Mama J insisted.

"Oh, you don't know my Tanzy. We're changing your reservations and putting you on her flight. Catch up with her and make the switch in flight. She'll probably realize the mistake in her reservations once she arrives in Costa Rica, then she'll give us a call and we'll book her the next flight out of there, on our dime, of course, and she'll not be any the wiser."

"Why do I have a sinking feeling in the pit of my stomach about this?" What I felt was more than bad indigestion. This scenario was a piping hot mess and I had a full-on fire burning in my gut. Beginning an operation with this type of mix-up was surely going to lead to disaster and get me killed in the process.

"She's Tanzy, but you're the *Fixer* and one of my best operatives. You can work a mission and fix anything and any situation. If anyone can straighten this out, it's you. Look, she has been trying to get into the business for a few years now. If you need to, let her think she's running the operation, that this is her test and you followed her to make sure everything went smoothly. She never has to leave Liberia Airport because you'll put her on the return flight as soon as you retrieve the fob.

"Yes, ma'am," I answered. What more could I say?

Chapter 3
Tanzy's Travels, livin' life and lovin' it!

T<i>anzy</i>

The phone chimed, letting me know my Uber driver was nearby. I gave my luggage one final perusal, roving my eye to make sure all the essentials were there. This was a five-day trip, but I wanted to be prepared for everything and probably overpacked a bit. My carry-on and the open pocketbook leaned against the suitcase. I reached over to zip everything but stumbled on an errant shoe and landed on the bed. The movement popped the bags in the air and the contents tumbled, including the bedazzled luggage fob. The gems adorning the sides flickered as they tumbled in the air. I'd almost forgotten about the thing.

"I think you would make the perfect identifier for my luggage at the airport baggage claim."

I filled in the information on the back, name, phone, and email, hooked it to the handle of my bag, hefted it off the bed, and dragged it to the front door, before placing them just outside on the front porch. I took a picture with my phone and made an entry in my notepad for the blog caption.

Coming up with the best opening for my blog was a struggle. I wanted something catchy, something fun that everyone would remember. Like, *Hello, my fellow adventurers, let's check this new place out.* Uhg, too many words. Then I changed it to *Tanzy's Travels, a sistah's journey abroad: Lovin' Life and Livin' It!* Ach, it's too long. There was a lot of brain power needed to cycle through these iterations. Finally, I cut it down to *Tanzy's Travels, lovin' life and livin' it!* The post was short, sweet, and finished just right as the Uber pulled up.

Hello, adventurers, this is your girl Tanzy T from DC making a break for the border.
First things first, pack your bag and don't forget the essentials.
We're heading for Liberia!

Dulles Airport was thirty miles away and always an hour with traffic. Doesn't seem fair but there you have it. The check-in for the flight to Liberia was smooth but security was its usual nightmare of long lines. The X-ray belt never failed to catch the edge of my carry-on. This time was no different. At least the handle survived most of the way intact and was usable. I wore slip-on sneakers to avoid the laces getting caught as well.

The plane was full so Mama J had to give me an aisle seat. I learned a long time ago to stop making my own reservations. Things tended to work out better when the plane reservations were created by professionals. Back when I was making my own arrangements, I'd end up in the strangest cities and airports. It stressed Mama J to the max trying to untangle my reservation woes. She finally insisted I go through her; if nothing else, she would have peace of mind. There was the added benefit of no longer needing to triple-check my tickets to make sure everything was okay.

We were over halfway through the flight when I looked up to see Phil walking down the aisle. He did say he was going to Liberia, but I did not realize he would be traveling on the same aircraft. Of course, that probably meant he was on some spy business. I briefly wondered what it was, then he flashed a forty-watt smile at me and all thoughts slipped loose from my brain, vanishing into thin air.

His gaze connected with mine and I plastered a grin on my face. Goodness, he was tall and fine. All smooth, caramel skin, clean-shaven, and close-cropped brown hair. His shirt stretched full with broad shoulders and thick abs. Describing him as drool-worthy seemed almost too simplistic. He was a cool sip of water on a hot, steamy summer night. Just my kind of drink.

I took a deep breath to calm down. He winked and spoke first.

"Hello, Tanzy, what a surprise to run into you."

"Hi, Phil, Mama J didn't tell me we were on the same flight. I guess she must keep things confidential."

"I didn't realize you were on board as well. I got up to stretch my legs and spotted you sitting here."

His voice was smooth as warm butter. Mesmerizing

too. I could talk to him all night long. "I'm glad you did. Is this trip for pleasure or business?" I was pretty sure it was business because Mama J's spies were always working, but the question came out anyway. Sort of a conversation starter.

"Some business but mostly pleasure," came the vague response. "How about you?"

"I've created a travel blog. This is my inaugural trip." I was so proud of how confident I sounded. This venture was a big step for me and even though I sounded positive, butterflies continued to flutter in my stomach anytime I described it.

His smile lit up the cabin. "Sounds interesting. I'll have to follow you."

"Sure thing, can I text you when we land?" Didn't think for a second he would give me his digits but, you never know.

"Here's my number," he offered.

He fished inside his pocket and produced a business card. Smooth as silk, this one. I mean, who carries business cards anymore these days? "Thanks."

"Contact me while you are in Liberia. Maybe we can have dinner."

Oh, my goodness, did he just ask me out? "I will. Just as soon as I get settled."

"What's your hotel?"

My mind went blank. I'd glanced at the itinerary briefly after I got home and stuffed it in the side of my carry-on.

"No worries, you can tell me later."

LOST IN LIBERIA

He was standing right under the compartment where I'd stowed my carry-on. "My bag is right above you. Can you hand it to me?"

"Are you sure? It can wait until we land."

"Not a problem, mine is the red one."

He followed my instructions and extracted the bag. He had an odd look on his face like there was something amiss.

"Anything wrong?"

"No, it's just that the handle looks pretty chewed up."

"Yeah, these security scanners are wicked machines. My carry-ons take a heavy hit every time I go through one."

"Ah, well, hopefully, you didn't have something hanging off of it like that glitzy new fob we both picked up from the travel agency." He seemed genuinely concerned.

He handed the bag over to me and I rooted around in the outer pocket until I found the right papers. "What? That blinged-out fob? I put it on my luggage. Come to think of it, my bag usually gets chewed up as well. What did you do with yours?"

He looked stunned for a moment, then his face returned to normal. "I uhm, put it on my carry-on."

"That's a good idea too, but I decided all that glam would be hard to miss at the luggage carousel." I found the itinerary and read the instructions. "Here it is, says I'm staying at the Pajaro Paradise Resort." The name sounded strange to me once I looked at it. It sounded Latin. I'd expected a hotel with more of an African name.

"Something wrong? I've heard of it. Really nice place. It's up the road from my hotel."

"Well, this is an odd name for a hotel in Liberia, Africa. It sounds almost Caribbean."

"Did you say Africa?" He looked amused.

"Yes, I did."

"Uhm, we're going to Liberia, Costa Rica."

My heart kicked into a heavy staccato beat. This felt like one of my colossal travel mix-ups, except I found it hard to believe. This trip was not booked by me, so I couldn't have made the mistake. "No, you're wrong. The flight attendant said when we took off, 'welcome aboard the flight to Liberia.' Even the time in the air sounded correct."

"Yes, the airport of Liberia is in Costa Rica. I believe if you were heading to the country in Africa, she would have said something like, 'welcome aboard the flight to Monrovia.' I think that's the city where most of the flights to Liberia go. They usually announce the airport names on the flight."

"Are you telling me there are two Liberias in the world?"

"Yes, one is the city and the other one is the country."

"Oh God, this can't be happening. Not again." I hated sounding like a five-year-old, but going through the agency was supposed to keep this sort of thing from happening to me.

LOST IN LIBERIA

The flight attendant came by passing out the immigration landing cards.

"Miss, what country are we landing in?"

"Ma'am, you're going to Costa Rica." She handed me the card. "Be sure to fill this out before we land. We'll be on the ground in about forty-five minutes."

I grabbed her hand. "You don't understand. I can't be on this flight!"

Chapter 4

Phil

The fob was hidden in my pocket ready to make the switch. When I saw the mangled strap, I thought the worst. Of course, when she explained the actual location of her fob, I was even more alarmed. Mama J had packed a lot of tech into the thing and now it sat below us in a questionable state. I would have to figure out how to fix it in the field. This also meant that I would have to string her along until we reached the ground and baggage claim. The problem was, I really liked Tanzy. Those big brown eyes captured my heart every time she gazed at me. I wanted to kiss her in the worst way. She was beautiful, funny, and sweet. She was also feisty and smart. So maybe she was a bit clumsy and, yes, her luck was not the best, but she had a genuinely good spirit. Mama J was right, she did not belong in our line of business, yet here she was about to get swept along.

"Look, Tanzy, don't worry about the flight. I'm sure Mama J will put you on a return flight. We can give her a call as soon as we land.

LOST IN LIBERIA

Her expression touched me. She honestly didn't know she was going to the wrong side of the world. I should have insisted on intercepting her and retrieving the fob before she boarded the flight.

"That's not the problem, Phil. No matter what I do, no matter how hard I try, crazy things happen to me. I put on a good face and act like these things are normal but I'm only kidding myself."

My God, she was killing me. I almost spilled the beans about knowing she was on the wrong flight and Mama J's idea of letting it happen anyway. She looked so disgusted with herself and sad, that I didn't want to add to her distress. "Don't say that. This cannot possibly be your fault. I'm sure we can fix it once we are on the ground."

"No, you don't understand. I hear the sly comments they make about me being a walking disaster, or if Calamity Jane were black and had a sister, she would look like me, or my all-time favorite, if it weren't for bad luck, I'd have no luck at all."

I opened my mouth but nothing came out.

"You see, even you're at a loss for words," she continued. "If anything goes wrong for any of my family members, they call it the Tanzy effect. If it's really bad, they'll say they've been Tanzied. Do you know what it's like being the reason for all the bad luck for an entire family?" She sat back and shook her head. "This is why they won't let me near the agency. And don't shake your head, you know what I'm talking about."

I froze. She was right, she was referring to the spy

organization they run in the back offices. My first instinct was to deny the very existence of the place. She saw right through my deception. The hurt in her eyes bore straight through my heart. It was impossible for me to move or even say something to clarify the situation. She motioned for me to lean closer.

"We can fix the flight and send me home, but we can't fix me. I'm bad luck Betty on a good day. I figured if I did the blog, people would see the real me."

With each passing moment, she made it difficult for me to keep my promise to see her onto the return flight.

The flight attendant came by and motioned toward me. She was tall with short, cropped hair and sun-kissed skin. "Sir, you'll have to take your seat. We'll be landing soon."

"Tanzy, cheer up. You'll get to do your blog and I'm sure it will be a big success."

She pinned me with red-rimmed brown eyes. "I sure hope so. Thanks for stopping and listening to my rambling."

******

Immigration was a cattle call with all of us foreign travelers queuing in a long line. I was ahead of Tanzy and cleared customs before her. This gave me enough time to make a call to Mama J.

"Mama's Travel Agency, call us if ya just gotta go. How may I help you?" Mama J answered.

"This is Fixer. I've landed and was unable to make the switch in flight."

LOST IN LIBERIA

"Where did she put it?"

"On her luggage. I have to wait until we get to baggage claim now."

"Thousands of dollars in tech traveling in the cargo hold. Why am I not surprised?" Mama J said with a groan.

I felt the need to defend Tanzy. "It's disguised as a luggage tag. So, putting it on her bag kind of makes sense."

"We were working on short notice and had to use what was available," she growled. "Just make the switch. Her return ticket is ready for her. She is on a flight that leaves in a few hours. Make sure she's on it."

"You don't want to use the option of letting her think she's leading a mission?"

"Heavens no. We need this to succeed and can't afford any slipups. The way things happen around her, this mission would fail before it started. We just got intel that the agent you are covering is about to be exposed. We need you on the ground and placing the device on the item that we are delivering to your hotel. You're the Fixer, now work your magic."

"Yes, ma'am."

My orders were clear. Swap out her fob, get her on the next plane smoking, and begin the operation. It all sounded so cut and dry. I found Tanzy by the baggage carousel. The other passengers milled about, packed into the small space by the luggage belt. My bag was one of the first ones off. Time moved on, the crowd thinned as more and more of them retrieved their luggage.

"Tanzy, yours should be off pretty soon," I pointed out.

"I'm sure it will be. It'll come off in one piece or another." She sounded resigned.

The belt stopped after one last lone bag slid by. "This is the last one. Is it yours?"

"No. Just wait a few minutes."

"Tanzy, there are no more. That's why the belt stopped."

She raised one finger as if she were a sage instructing a pupil. "Wait one more minute."

I was about to suggest we go to the lost luggage office when the claxon sounded, then the belt jerked and began to move. A few seconds later, a blue bag slid down the shoot. It was in pretty bad shape. Clothing protruded out all four sides, and scratches marred its pebble surface. A belt ran around the middle barely holding the contents inside. The handle with the fob was missing.

"Where's the handle?" I hoped I did not sound as alarmed as I felt.

"Don't worry. I had this happen before."

We wrestled the bag off of the belt and settled it on the floor. A stray sock flopped out the side.

Tanzy turned the bag around and pointed. On the flip side was the handle, taped to its flank with some airport tape. The fob was nestled underneath. "See, they taped it to the underside. Everything is here though."

"Are you sure?" I was dubious.

"Yeah, this actually looks pretty good. I've seen worse. At least my underwear is not falling out. Do you know how embarrassing it is to see your panties and bra taped to the underside of your bag?"

"No, I've not had that experience."

She gave me the sweetest and saddest smile. She leaned close and planted a kiss on my cheek, making my heart skip a beat. My head turned and our lips connected. Electricity, molten fire, then fireworks exploded in my head. The sensation settled to low heat and sweet brown sugar. We lingered far too long before pulling away.

"Sorry, I was aiming for your cheek."

I didn't want her to think it was her fault. "No worries. It was me. I moved." *Why did I sound like a schoolboy after his first kiss?*

"Uhm, okay," she began. "Thanks for staying with me until my bag arrived. I'm sure you've been in contact with Mama J."

"Tanzy…" I felt like a heel. Everyone at the agency tiptoed around her and tried to keep her in the dark. But clearly, she was in the know and aware of our activities.

"No, no. It's okay. She texted me and said my return ticket is waiting for me at check-in. This will be yet another story they will use as fodder in the epic unlucky tales of Tanzy the Terrible."

I didn't know how she wormed her way under my skin. But she did. I was the agent in the field and could make judgment calls should I deem it necessary. Escorting Tanzy to her new flight was a direct order. Yet somehow option B kept intruding on my conscience. Besides, what harm could it be if she tagged along?

"Uhm, Tanzy, I was given different orders."

"What do you mean?"

The handle and fob pulled away from the side of the bag, the tape wasn't that strong to begin with. My mind was very clear on what I had to do, the orders were precise. One look at her big brown eyes and my heart took over.

The fob glinted on my hand, an orange, red, and green crystal rainbow. "You were not on the plane by accident. Besides, you know Mama J never makes a mistake."

"What are you saying?" Her eyes lit up.

"This is your first mission. I'm here to guide you. This fob has tech embedded in it that will help our operative in the field." There was a bit more to it than that. I had to MacGyver an electronic device back to life and install it into another device.

"What?" she squealed.

I turned the fob over and pointed to a tiny switch hidden under the rhinestones. "All we have to do is push this, the light on the top turns green and it's ready for the transfer."

I handed the fob to her. She flipped it over a couple of times. "Is the light supposed to be red before we push it?"

What an odd question. She showed me the end and the light. Sure enough, it was red. "Dammit, this means it's malfunctioning. The switch must have been damaged when they broke the handle."

"What can we do?" she asked.

"Turn it off."

LOST IN LIBERIA

The red light indicated internal damage. If not repaired, the mission would be scuttled before it started. The fob had to be deactivated. I pressed the hidden button, but the light remained red. The hard reset was on the reverse side, its dimpled indentation inside the travel agency logo. One press later and the light faded away.

I exhaled. "It's off but we may have to move quickly to maintain any chance of fixing it.

"What do we do now?" she asked.

The answer was clear but I remembered this was supposed to be her op.

"It's up to you, you're in charge."

Chapter 5

*Hello, adventurers, this is your girl Tanzy T from DC.
I've landed in paradise on the wrong side of the world!
Y'all ain't gonna believe this but there are two Liberias and I found the other one.
I see palm trees, sun-drenched blue skies, a tropical breeze, and a cold drink in the near future.
Oh well, might as well explore Costa Rica while I'm here!
#lovinlifeandlivinit*

*T*anzy

Oh, hell no, he did not just lay the whole 'you're in charge' thing on me. *Eek!*

Just like that, I'd been handed something I'd always wanted. I, Tanzy James, was in charge of an operation. My legs moved in a little two-step in the middle of the Liberia Airport baggage area. Two steps right, two left, one front, one back, and spin. Had to dance out my elation.

"Calm down. Remember, we've got to keep ourselves low-key. Don't draw attention," Phil admonished.

"Sorry about that. Couldn't help myself. First things first, let's get out of here."

LOST IN LIBERIA

Made my first decision for my first mission and no catastrophe occurred. Let the family think what they want, I could do this job as well as any of them.

From the smile on his face, Phil seemed happy with my choice. There should be a law against his smile, he could brighten the darkest room. "I think that's a perfectly reasonable suggestion. Let's go," he said.

I flipped out my phone to take a selfie video of me in front of the *Welcome to Liberia* marquee. Flashed my signature two-fingered peace sign, wagged my brows, and sauntered off toward the exit. Phil picked up the pace, clearly not wanting to be in the vid. I jogged to catch up, all the while typing up my thoughts, ending with my hashtag for lovin' life.

"What are you posting?" Phil asked.

"My blog. I'm not going to drop my new business just because we are on a case. Plus, I gotta keep up my cover as a tourist. Don't want everyone to know I'm here on spy business."

"Pipe it down. Remember, we have to keep a low profile." His voice was low and harsh.

"Okay, okay. Chill, we got this," was my equally low reply.

In one fluid motion, he lifted the handlebar on my damaged bag. Shockingly it slid free, the wheels were intact and the bag rolled effortlessly behind him, gapping edges, flapping clothes and all. The bag's condition did not seem to faze him one bit. He led us outside to a line of waiting taxis. It was hot and humid; the warm breeze only served to make me wish for a cold margarita. Phil spoke a few words in Spanish to a burly driver whose cab stood ready at the front of the line.

"*Donde quieres ir*?" our driver inquired.

Phil leaned over. "Where to, boss? Your hotel or mine?"

What an offer. Never thought I would hear a question like that come from his lips. "Your hotel." I was a bit breathy on the reply. Had to clear my throat to rein it in. "We can work on the fob there before you take me to mine. Or, better yet, let's see if we can switch my reservations to your hotel."

Decision number two completed without a single incident. I was on a roll.

The cab was a yellow mini-van driven by a sweaty, t-shirt-wearing man named Paulo. He had an infectious gapped tooth smile, and a broad chin that sported five days' worth of stubble. We peeled out of the airport at warp speed, taking corners a bit too close. I clutched the sides of my seat but still managed to rub legs with Phil. A glorious shiver ran up and down the right side of my body when his hard muscular body met mine. His gaze smoldered and my breath caught. He broke a few laws with that look and I wanted him to break a few more. His whole vibe was lethal and needed to be on a registry somewhere. The cab shifted and our bodies parted, giving me a few moments to think.

"The cabbie seems to be in a bit of a hurry." Was that my voice? All husky and breathy? I needed to power down my batteries in the worst way.

"I paid him to get us to the hotel as fast as possible."

LOST IN LIBERIA

"Of course, that makes sense."

The drive to the coast was too fast in my mind. Any reason to cozy up to Phil, even a speeding car, was a good one, but I would have preferred more time to savor the ride. We arrived in a wooded area full of cozy guesthouses and small hotels. Between the trees, the white caps of the Pacific sparkled in the afternoon sun. People lounged on blankets or dodged in and out of the surf.

"Wow, who knew it was like this?" I whispered.

"It is gorgeous but I guess this was not what you were expecting."

I had to admit even to myself. The Tanzy effect landed me smack-dab in the middle of a Central America trip instead of Africa. Yeah, this was way different. "No, it is not. Especially since I'm not supposed to be here. But I think I can pivot and make the most out of this trip."

"What's your plan?" he asked.

I thought about it for a moment. First things first, get the fob working. Also, I needed more information. "Let's fix the thing and you tell me our objective."

Phil hesitated as if he were weighing his words. "Okay," he finally said in hushed tones. "This is for your ears only. I'm the Fixer."

"The what?" I could take that statement in many ways. Did he turn a wrench, hack a computer, or make people disappear? I wanted to hear more.

"I fix things. If there's an issue that needs my specialty, I fly in and take care of it."

He was not telling me everything. Curiosity brought out more questions. "By taking care of it, you mean you repair a car or make a human problem disappear?"

"A bit of both," was his cautious reply.

"I see," I said, then reconsidered. "No, I don't."

"That's pretty much all I can say right now. But what I can tell you is that we're here to track down one of our operatives here in Coco Beach and…"

"You mean they have a Coco Beach down here too?" I interrupted. Too many same named locations for my tastes, but who was I to judge?

"Yes, they do." His smile was infectious. "We need to locate him and take this microchip embedded in the fob and give it to him."

I was, after all, an IT specialist. In spite of what my former employers said. So, this kind of operation was right up my alley. "Microchips are small, how do you intend to do the transfer?"

"I'm placing it in another package. The kit is in the backpack. They're delivering the package to the hotel."

"Cool, this is my jam. Should be a smooth operation." I was excited.

Hotel Bosque loomed ahead, nestled between the trees and looking more like a fancy tree house than a resort. The car rolled to a smooth stop under a canopy of leaves that filtered the afternoon sun into a diffused light. The façade was a soft dreamy pallet in tropical colors of oranges, yellows, and blues. A short flight of steps led up to an open lobby. Comfy couches dotted the lobby, the registration desk was tucked off in the corner as if to remain unobtrusive but still retain its function.

"*Buenos Dias Señor. Tienes equipaje?*" the porter greeted and asked us if we had luggage.

"*Si, ella tambien.*" Phil handed him what was left of my bag, then motioned for me to proceed up the steps.

"I have a good feeling about this trip," he began. "I really don't believe in luck, be it bad or good. Things happen and we make adjustments accordingly…"

My foot caught on the last riser and down I went. It was my typical slow-motion trip and fall which usually ended in a glorious sprawl on my belly. Except this time, strong arms wrapped around my waist, pulling me upright, encircling me close. I found myself surrounded by a whole lot of Phil, sort of a Phil blanket. His scent was intoxicating, cinnamon and musk with a hint of chicory that he puts in his coffee. His chest was broad and rock hard, dark hairs curled between the gap in his shirt. His gaze was intense, his lips raised in a half smile as if something amused him.

"We'll have none of that, Miss James," he soothed. "How about we see if they have a room available for you? It'll make getting around the city easier."

My head was swimming. I was curled inside massive arms and tucked up against a rock-hard chest. Standing this close to tall, dark and Phil was surreal, almost as if this were another life, not my own. *Be still, my beating heart.*

I concentrated on keeping my face and voice neutral. "It's part of my new plan. I'll text Mama J to have her cancel the other hotel."

At the front desk, a young lady dressed in an aqua-colored suit greeted us. "*Hola, Señor y Señora.* Welcome to the Bosque Hotel. How may I help you?"

"Do you have a room available for the next few nights?" I asked. My fingers were crossed as I prayed away the Tanzy effect.

"We do have a suite on the upper floor."

Dear Lord, the word suite sounded expensive "Oh, I don't know…"

"It should work just fine," Phil interjected. He placed a silver card in her hand.

"Phil, I'm reimbursing you," I insisted.

"Agreed."

Chapter 6

Phil

The more I was around Tanzy, the deeper she burrowed into my heart. Her smile, a little crooked with a lot of sass, lit her face. Cinnamon highlights dusted each lock of hair catching the sunlight every time she moved. Her skin was a smooth chocolate brown, and she seemed to prefer dark cherry red lipstick. Her laugh was low and husky, sort of made me think of sultry tropical nights. If I was not careful, I'd botch this job daydreaming about Tanzy. She was different from the other women I knew. Something about her added spice to an otherwise routine day for me. I really was not sure what it was, but inviting her along for this assignment seemed right to me in spite of Mama J's dire warnings. How could her presence possibly be wrong?

We promised to take a couple of hours to change before we tackled the repair work on the fob. I chose a cold shower. Its spray helped clear my mind and cool me down. Could not afford to lose my concentration as the next few hours were crucial to our success. My phone rang a soft unobtrusive chime that most times only I could hear. It was Mama J. She probably called to tell me off for not putting Tanzy on the return flight.

"This is Fixer."

"Yes, I know that. What I don't know is why you changed my orders?"

Here we go. "It was a judgment call. I decided to have her on this mission."

"She's a walking disaster waiting to happen. Get her out of there."

That sounded ominous. "The mission will go off without a hitch. We haven't had any problems so far." I'd decided the luggage snafu could happen to anyone. The airlines moved thousands of bags every day. One was always bound to be damaged.

"It's your funeral in more ways than one."

"What's that supposed to mean?" I was not easily alarmed, but her voice took on a deeper, more ominous tone.

"As you know, we had to wait until you got in the country before we gave you your target."

This conversation was not heading in a good direction. The bundle of muscles above my eye twitched then settled down. "You might as well tell me so I can get on with this operation. Who am I meeting?"

There was a long pause before she continued. "Sunshine."

My heart skipped a beat. The muscles above my eye contracted painfully. I rubbed the area but was unable to stop the inevitable dance of pain that radiated in my brow. I got up and paced the floor, began counting my way through my breathing exercises to slow my pulse. Anything to cut through the knot of emotions that name brought forth.

"Jesus, Mama J, you want me to rendezvous with my ex?"

"Fixer, you're a professional. You can handle this...even with Tanzy in tow."

This was a disaster through and through and I refused to blame Tanzy. Though having her along complicated matters in the worst way. "You should have told me I was meeting Sunshine before I left."

"We didn't have all of the intel other than you were needed in Costa Rica by a certain day. It would not have mattered anyway. You are the only one who can swap out the chip embedded in the fob."

The now inoperable fob.

I rubbed my forehead and dug into my bag for a Tylenol. Images of the last time I saw Sunshine flashed through my mind. The explosion catapulted me over the sea wall. The blue sky mixed in with the red flames of the fire as I tumbled end over end. The splash of water as I landed in the sea. The cool sensation of oblivion as I sank beneath the waves.

My old life ended that day. I woke up in a hospital vowing never to get emotionally involved with another operative again and most importantly, never laying eyes on Sunshine again.

"Fixer? Did I lose you?"

Mama J's voice grew concerned. I did check out for a

moment, the pain of memories long buried temporarily shut my mind down. I heard not one word she said.

"I'm here. Just tell me what you want me to fix, then I'm outta here." My voice was rough. The thought of seeing Sunshine again rattled me more than I wanted to admit. I dug into my bag and found something to knock the edge off the drum thumping at my temple. Massaging the area was not working.

"I won't beat around the bush. I know you two have a history, but this couldn't be helped."

"Describing what we had as history is the understatement of the century," I grated.

"Don't you get smart with me, young man. You asked to get back out in the field as soon as you were able. You knew there was a possibility you two would run into each other."

Sunshine was in a completely different sector of activity than me. There was no way we would ever cross paths. "I don't see how. She handles the info you want to acquire by passing off gifts as part of medical intervention. There is nothing in my job description that says I fix her type of gifts. I mean, they're sex toys, for Christ's sake."

"You're not there to fix one, you're there to put a chip in one." Her reply was lofty as if there was a big difference between the two.

"You can't possibly be serious."

"I am. A messenger is delivering the package to your hotel this afternoon. The fob is offline for some odd reason. No doubt something to do with Tanzy. We need you to turn it back on so we can finish loading the data. Once that's done, you take the chip out of the back compartment and load it into the package. Then deliver it to Sunshine."

A knock on the door sent my jangled nerves to the stratosphere. I jumped and lost my grip on the phone. It tumbled through the air as I fumbled to catch it, missed it completely, and it landed with a low thud on the tile floor. Thankfully, the case saved it from breaking. I scooped it up and covered the speaker.

"Who is it?" I yelled at the door.

"It's Tanzy," came her muffled reply. "I was downstairs when a package arrived for you. I brought it up. Can I come in?"

"Mama J, I'll get back with you later." I pressed the red button and disconnected the call without waiting for her reply.

A few steps took me across the room to open the door. Tanzy stood in the hallway wearing a tight orange top with matching capri pants that hugged every curve she owned, red lipstick, matching kitten pumps, and a broad smile. In her hand was a box wrapped in brown paper addressed to me. She held it up as if presenting a prized package.

"It sloshes a little but is lightweight. What do you think it is?"

Not in a million years would I have imagined a beautiful woman dressed like the devil, smelling as sweet as a summer rose, would deliver a sex toy to my hotel room door. But then again, maybe this was the true

Tanzy effect. She rendered me mute. I swallowed once, then twice, before I found my voice. "Why don't you come in?"

"I think I will."

Her heel caught in a small hole in the tile. She stumbled. The package popped out of her hand and was airborne before either one of us could react. I caught her, concentrating hard on not connecting with her breasts that stretched her top and my imagination to its breaking point. The box landed with a plop and slid across the room.

"Jeez, I hope that wasn't fragile."

"So do I, Tanzy, so do I."

LOST IN LIBERIA

Chapter 7

Hello, adventurers, this is your girl Tanzy T from DC.
One word about a vacation outfit!
Go bold, go tight, go orange.
Add hot shoes and you have yourself the perfect vacay ensemble.
Watch the men stare when you enter a room!
#lovinlifeandlivinit

*T*anzy

The look on Phil's face was priceless, equal parts surprise mixed in with smoldering appreciation for my outfit. Bringing him the package was completely unplanned. I was downstairs taking selfies for my next blog post when the box arrived. The nice man at the desk agreed to let me bring it up to Phil. Clumsy me, I wasn't paying attention to where I placed my foot, my shoe caught and I almost did a face-plant right there in front of him. Luckily, he caught me. He wrapped those big arms around me and pulled me in close, mashing my bosom to his chest. The embers of heat and fire were in his gaze. He studied my face so intently, I half expected he would swoop down and plant a hot kiss. Instead, he set me on my feet and held me at arm's length.

He retrieved the box and placed it on a small table.

"Aren't you going to open it?"

"Not yet, we need to get the fob working first." Something about the package seemed to upset him.

He pulled a small case out of his backpack and returned to the table. Wires, probes, and a multimeter were neatly stacked inside. He arranged them in order on the table. A specially insulated pad came out next. I recognized it as something used to minimize static discharge that could possibly fry a component.

"Take a seat and I'll pull out the fob."

He slid the fob out of his pocket and set it on the pad. Jeweled crystals glinted off the sunlight that streamed through the open window. It was really quite beautiful and artfully designed. The whole idea of hiding the tech in the thing was brilliant. It passed through security and no one was the wiser.

"Okay, let's take a look," Phil said.

With a flat blade, he pried open the case, exposing the inner circuitry, a small control board with its diodes, resistors, and wires. Yep, this was my jam and I leaned in for a closer look.

"I see where there's a break in the wire." I pointed out the location. A charred area surrounded the spot. It was hard to miss.

"Good catch. Let me repair that first. I don't see much else, so this should run smoothly."

He reached over with a micro-soldering device that also appeared out of his travel case. I half wondered if he had a bottle of vodka in there as well. I noticed he was missing a crucial piece to the setup. My hand was out to grab his wrist before I could think of a better way to slow him down. "No, wait. You forgot something."

The muscle above his right eye twitched but he remained calm.

"What?"

I'd been trained on these kinds of circuits and they drilled into me the first rule for this kind of work. "You must put on your ground wire before you start. Otherwise, you might fry the whole board."

His features flashed several emotions, they ran the gamut from his initial irritation to thoughtfulness, then gratitude. His lips bowed up into a sheepish grin and he nodded in appreciation. "You do know your stuff. You're right, I should ground myself."

In the case was an additional zippered compartment. He pulled out a wristband with its grounding wire and slipped it on. He clipped the wire to ground and continued with the repair. Once complete, the two halves of the fob were closed. Phil pushed the small button decorated like a blue crystal, and the green light at the end came to life. Part one of our work was complete.

Phil opened his phone and made a call. "Okay, the fob is back on. Start transmitting now."

It was fascinating watching him work. He was laser-focused and in his element. The muscle above his eye never moved, not once. I realized I was watching the Fixer in action and had a feeling that this was a special privilege not accorded to many.

Soon the light faded to pale green and began to blink on and off. He turned the fob over and opened a tiny compartment. Inside lay a small circular disk.

"Listen, Tanzy, we must now install this disk in the item they delivered this afternoon. He placed his hand on the box, closed his eyes, and took a deep breath. When he opened them, he seemed resolved about his next move. He pulled a knife out of his bottomless case, then deftly cut open the paper wrapper on the box and opened the sides. A sealed plastic container lay in the interior. Inside was a wooden object that floated in a viscous liquid.

Phil donned plastic gloves he retrieved from his bag. "Don't get any of this liquid on your hands," he said.

"What is it? Why can't we touch it?"

"I can't say. Just keep clear of the stuff."

He broke the seal. The scent of sandalwood and sage filled the air.

"At least it smells nice," I noted.

He extracted a small wooden object. It was ebony in color and glistened in the light.

"Is that oil all over it?"

"Yes, essential oil infused with CBD and performance enhancers. Stay clear of it."

I thought I'd heard it all. "Performance enhancers? You mean as in sexual performance? Really? This looks look like a fancy lampshade finial. And did they bedazzle the end of it?" The knob of the wood was encrusted with red crystals. A hole ran through the jeweled side.

LOST IN LIBERIA

"What is it?" The question came out of my mouth way too fast.

"Would you believe this is a butt plug?" came his reply along with a look of disgust.

We both sat there in silence for a minute. I needed to process what he was saying and what my lying eyes were seeing. This was not some fancy decoration for a piece of furniture. This was a sex toy. When the realization finally dawned on me, I stood up so fast the chair toppled over.

"A BUTT PLUG? No way, let me see it."

Okay, I was not the most adventurous when it came to escapades in the bed. I was pretty boring and did not venture too far away from the basic positions. Utilizing props and tools was not my thing. It wasn't that I disapproved or anything like that, just never had an opportunity to test-drive one, or a partner interested in giving it a go. I'd seen dildoes before, but never a butt plug. So, to see one in person for the first time was a bit exciting. "Can I hold it?"

Phil's eye began to twitch again. In the short time I was around him, it seemed to me his twitch indicated that he was uncomfortable with the situation. This was a toy and from what I could see, someone went to a lot of trouble to soak it in oils and glam it up. The question was, why did it bother him?

"Phil, it's okay, we're adults here and this is a mission. The agency must have a good reason for wanting that chip in this…uhm…" I had trouble getting the words out of my mouth without giggling.

"Sex toy?" he finished the thought.

"Yeah." A tiny chuckle escaped my lips before I could pull it back.

"If you must know, my talents are better served disarming bombs, fixing escape vehicles, or even hacking into computers. Planting a chip in one of these is a bit…" He paused. "Let's just say they could have sent someone else." He looked distraught over the fact that he had to work on it.

He acted like the plug was dangerous and the oil was radioactive. I could not imagine something that smelled so pleasant could be bad for you. I reached out and snagged the plug from him. Oil covered my hands, soaking into the pores of my skin, which tingled with a warm sensation. I liked the feeling and could not understand Phil's aversion to it.

Phil dashed to the bathroom and came back with a towel. "Here, wipe your hands quickly. You don't know what this substance will do."

"Calm down. This is a lot of drama for a butt plug." I could not shake the feeling that something else bothered him though. I ignored the towel and rubbed my hands together to soak up the oil. The resulting smooth skin was a delight. He was overreacting for sure.

As far as I was concerned, a job still needed to be performed and I was perfectly capable of completing it. "Think of it this way. They did send someone else."

He raised an eyebrow but remained silent.

"They sent me. I know how to work with electronics." I pulled the ground wire assembly from his wrist and placed it on mine. "I'll put it in. It's my operation after all. Take off your gloves, you won't be needing them."

His face went from shock to full-on alarm in one fluid motion. "No, Tanzy, let me. You misunderstood what I was saying."

"I don't think so." I held the plug with one hand and turned it back and forth. The thing had some weight to it. Why someone would want to plug their ass with something this heavy was beyond me, but to each his own. A tiny switch was located, hidden in the first row of crystals. I flipped it and the damned thing began to vibrate. I nearly dropped the plug but caught it in mid-tumble. The color drained from Phil's face.

Clearly, this was not the way to open it. "Where's the catch on this thing?"

"Tanzy, I must insist. Let me fix it." He reached for it and I pulled away from him.

"Phil, I'll do it. Now show me how to open it."

"Tanzy," Phil began, but I cut him off.

"This is my op and that's an order."

Phil glared but remained quiet. My hands were completely covered in sage-smelling oil, making the plug a bit slippery. I toggled the switch off and inspected it closer. There was a slit in the top, nestled between the crystals. "I think I found it."

He rooted around in his case and pulled out a magnifying glass and a small flat-blade screwdriver, smaller than the kind you use to repair glasses. At least he swallowed his objection and decided to help.

"Take your time and be careful," he advised. He

moved the glass into position. "I'll hold this so you can see it properly." He was the laser-focused Phil once again.

The magnification helped a lot. I was able to push the spot and slide out a small tray. This was surgical precision time and Phil made a great assistant. He produced tweezers for me to lift the disk out of the fob and place it into the tray. It took me a bit to get the tray closed but I finally pushed it home.

"Here, dab a small bead of this glue over the site." Phil held a silver tube in his hand.

"You're not worried that this will sink in and corrupt the disk?"

"This glue is my special formula designed to attach to the surface. You'll only need one drop.

I followed his instructions and placed the butt plug back on the rubber mat. "See, job done smooth as silk, and the work is completely covered."

He relaxed and sat back in his chair. "Not bad for your first time in the field fixer assignment," he said with a relieved chuckle. In one fluid motion, he placed the plug back in the oil and closed the lid. He failed to put the gloves back on and some of the oil reached his hand. "It's sealed and can go back in the box."

"How did you know it's supposed to be resubmerged?"

His expression closed into a blank stare. There were clearly aspects of his life he didn't want to share. "It's a long story. Suffice it to say that we must deliver it in its oils."

LOST IN LIBERIA

I placed the cap back on the tube and passed it to him. "Now, will you tell me what was really troubling you?"

His reaction would have been comical if he hadn't jerked his hand and connected with mine as I released the tube of glue. The cap slipped off on impact and a blob of glue squirted out where our hands collided.

"Oh no!" I yelled. I could feel the stuff spreading between our palms finding every crease and valley and welding them together.

Phil stared in horror at our entwined hands. His eye twitched a samba and his full kissable lips were clamped in a tight bow.

"Well, say something," I demanded.

"This is gonna take some time."

Chapter 8

*P*_{hil}

I've always prided myself on hiding my emotions. The tall, silent one who was efficient, precise, and completely closed off. Yet, somehow, Tanzy could read me like an open book, cover to cover, between each line and with a full glossary in the back. How the hell did this happen? Even worse, why was I considering an explanation of any kind?

The specially formulated oil that would dissolve the glue was in my supply case. A few quick steps to the bathroom with Tanzy and we were at the sink with the oil. The oil went over our combined palms but I had trouble getting it between them. "Tanzy, I'm going to turn your hand this way."

"Ouch. Not so hard," she complained.

"We have to move fast before it sets up."

"I think we're too late. It feels pretty damn well set up to me."

She was right. We were stuck fast. At this rate, it would take hours and several applications to dissolve the glue.

LOST IN LIBERIA

"So how long will this take for the oil to work?" she asked.

"A few hours. Why?"

"'Cause I gotta pee."

We were in the bathroom anyway, so why not?

"Okay, I'll turn around."

"That's nice but I need you to help me unzip my pants."

I could see the front of her pants and there was no zipper. "I don't see it."

"That's because it's in the back."

It took a lot of maneuvering before my free hand could reach the zipper and her free hand could pull her pants down. I never expected it to be so hard to get a woman out of her clothes. I turned away long enough for her to finish her business. She flushed and moved to the sink. We washed our hands together, of course. I realized that if I had to pick someone to be glued to, I could not have done better. I liked Tanzy, a lot, which meant we were probably doomed. My stiff demeanor and workaholic ways always seemed to kill a relationship. The only exception was Sunshine. She was just as much of a worker bee as me. To say we had a thing going was laughable considering the few times we were together. The job always seemed to take first priority.

"Phil, if we're stuck together, we might as well have dinner and a walk on the beach," Tanzy reasoned.

"Oh no, we need to stay in. Minimize our exposure." My basic instinct kicked in. Move like a ghost, show up, do the job, and get out. No distractions and don't let too many people see you.

"Why? Don't you like walking on the beach? Plus, I'm starved."

She was right. We'd been traveling all day without a break. The plug was set and repacked. There was not much more to do but eat and wait to go find Sunshine on the beach tomorrow. Of course, there was the little problem of unsticking our hands.

I was able to fold my fingers over hers. To a casual observer, it would look like we were holding hands. The hotel had an open floor plan with wide verandas that brought the outdoor space in. Trees swayed over the rails with the afternoon breeze. We could hear the sound of the surf rolling onto the beach. The cry of seagulls echoed against the sky. Monkeys chattered in the trees, insects buzzed in the bushes. All this added to the tree house vibe of the hotel.

We had an option of taking a wide sweeping staircase or the elevator. I led us to the elevator but met resistance when I reached for the down arrow.

"If you don't mind, I'd rather take the stairs," Tanzy said as she pulled my hand back.

"Why, what's the problem?"

"I know this sounds strange, but I don't have much luck with elevators."

There she goes with the luck thing. She is too hard on herself sometimes. "How so?"

"They tend to break when I get on them."

"Tanzy, that's ridiculous…"

LOST IN LIBERIA

She shook her head and held up our glued hands. "You're telling me you don't believe shit happens to me?"

As much as I hated to admit it, she had a point. "Okay then, stairs it is."

We backtracked to the staircase and made our way down to the ground floor and out to the lobby. We stopped by the desk to ask for directions to the dining room.

"Aren't you a cute couple?" Maria, the afternoon clerk, gushed. "You look so cute holding hands that way." She leaned closer and whispered, "I wish my boyfriend would hold my hands that way."

"Why, you're so sweet," Tanzy offered before I could object. "We just started dating. You know, young love. He just won't let me go. It's as if we're glued to each other. I can't even go to the bathroom without him holding my hand." She finished with a nervous laugh that was infectious.

Maria chuckled like Tanzy made the best couples joke in the world.

I was uncomfortable with the conversation and nudged Tanzy forward. "Which way to the dining room?" I interjected.

"Oh, it's down the stairs, then take the path to the right. It will lead you straight there."

Dining at Bosque Hotel was an open-air affair with canopies strategically placed to cover the tables and food. The buffet was clearly out of the question, so we sat in a far corner holding hands and gazing out at the surf. A waiter came by and took our order, carne asada, and fried plantains. It smelled heavenly when it arrived. I ate with my left hand, Tanzy with her right. I was not a southpaw and had a little trouble getting the food onto the fork initially. Eventually, I got the hang of it and the meal went smoothly.

"Phil, you gonna tell me what's really bothering you?"

"I swear, Tanzy, you're like a dog with a bone," I evaded the question.

"So I'm told. But here's the rub. We're glued together because of your reaction when I first brought it up. I figure, you owe me some stripe of an explanation." She raised her left hand and my right followed, still firmly glued.

"Fine, before you arrived with the box, I received a call from Mama J with the rest of my instructions." I paused to collect my thoughts. As a loner, it was hard to share my feelings and even harder to explain things.

"We have to rendezvous with an agent named Sunshine Sage."

"Okay, were will we meet her?"

"At a hotel about forty minutes south of here."

She went quiet and continued to eat her plantain. "Here's the thing," she started. "I'm going to assume Sunshine is a lady and you two had a thing going. Nothing else will explain your behavior."

Who was this woman? I was pretty sure she did not have a psychology degree. Yet, here she was drilling right through me and straight to the heart of the matter.

LOST IN LIBERIA

She even managed to make the whole affair seem childish. "Damn, you're good."

"No, I just watch people a lot."

"Yeah, but you were spot on. Let's take that walk now."

A short path lead through the trees and out to the beach. Soft sand, heated by the afternoon sun, spread before us. We both took off our shoes. Tanzy wiggled her feet in the sand, a big smile spreading across her face. "What's the name of this beach?"

"Hermosa Beach."

She beamed as she took in the view. "Nice. I love the feel of sand between my toes."

"I don't, it's a pain trying to scrub it all off afterward."

We walked hand in hand like any other couple except, we weren't a couple. We were stuck together.

"Phil, you are such a killjoy."

"That's what my exes used to say." God, she had me pegged. "Tanzy, am I that transparent?"

"Man, your back is stiffer than my mama's ironing board. You need to relax and live a little."

She was right, but I didn't know how. "I'm pretty sure I'm incapable of relaxing."

We strolled along the shore, chasing the ebb and flow of the tide, the water cooling the sting of the hot sand.

"Is that why Sunshine dumped you?"

Tanzy was not going to be happy without the rest of the story.

"No, not really. I mean…I don't know. We were

good for a while. Our jobs competed for our couple time mostly. I would fly off to exotic places to fix things or situations. She stayed back and fixed people, mostly men, and their sex lives. Then she tried to kill me."

"With bejeweled dildoes and play toys?"

"Those are the extra benefits. She a doctor who specializes in CBD products that either enhance the libido or work on erectile dysfunction. She became especially sought-after for the latter when she developed a potent formula."

"Wow, I can see that. Good for her." Tanzy stopped and stared at me. "Did she experiment on you?"

She touched the subject I loathed to talk about. So, I decided to sidestep it altogether. "No, but Mama J recruited her to get close to some rather nefarious businessmen here in Central America."

"And we're here to deliver that toy to her so she can plant it on someone."

"Someone who has a few kinks," I added.

"What time do we meet?

"Around noon tomorrow."

"Then we best hit the sack. Tomorrow will be a long day."

Tanzy turned toward the darkening horizon and inhaled a lungful of sea air. She pulled out her phone. "Here, take a few shots of me and the sunset. I've got a few thousand followers now and they are eager for a report."

I loved her spirit. Every day was an adventure. All we had to do was step outside and enjoy it. She posed for a few pictures and prepared her post. I marveled at how she did it with one hand when I needed to use both. We made our way back to the lobby and started up the steps.

"Whose room do we sleep in?" she asked.

I raised our entwined hands. She was right, we were still stuck and would have to share a bed. "My room. I can periodically put oil on our hands throughout the night."

Chapter 9

Hello, adventurers, this is your girl Tanzy T from DC.
Day one is complete.
Just look at this sunset sky all purple, orange, and deep blue
I had a lovely meal and capped off the evening with a walk on the beach.
Do you have someone to curl up with tonight?
Like and leave your comments.
#lovinlifeandlivinit

*T*anzy

We stopped by my room for my toothbrush and a change of clothes. I also grabbed my pajama bottoms as taking off my top would be a bit difficult while glued to Phil. We made it back to Phil's room, where we brushed our teeth and took care of personal stuff without a hitch, then Phil looked down at his sand-encrusted feet.

"Listen, do you mind if we sit in the shower and run the water to clean our feet?" Phil asked.

I had to admit, the sand would eventually bother me, especially the stuff between my toes. "Good idea."

There was no tub in the room. The shower was made with one of those rainfall faucets that sprinkled water directly from the center of the shower ceiling. We both stared up at it at a loss as to how to proceed. If we had a tub, we could sit on the side fully dressed and rinse ourselves. This shower setup meant we would get completely wet.

"What do you think?" I asked.

"There is a handheld piece to it. Let's strip down to our underwear. I'll rinse your legs and you rinse mine."

That sounded reasonable, except I was starting to feel the effects of the oils. I was not sure I would behave myself standing in the shower with a sexy man in his undies. "Okay, but make it quick."

In short order, we were back in the shower. I was glad I'd brought my matching underwear set. Hot red, lacy, and a little see-through. He turned on the water and changed the setting so the water flowed through the handset. Cool water blasted me right in the face before he grabbed the shower wand from its cradle and turned the spray away from me. My nipples hardened and my red underwear was wet and completely see-through.

"Oops, sorry," he apologized.

"No, you aren't," I teased.

"Here, sit on this ledge and I can soap your legs and feet."

The shower stall was tiled in a dark blue. A short ledge ran across the far side. Phil began by applying soap and sudsing my limbs. Oh boy was this sexy as hell. The feel of his hand running up then down to my toes was equal parts thrilling and sensual. I would let him do the rest of me if he were so inclined, but that would probably lead to other things we would best not explore.

Soon he finished and it was my turn to wash and rinse his legs. One-handed, no less. The soap went on fairly easily but I had trouble holding the shower wand. Water sluiced in all directions until I got it under control enough to finish the job.

I looked up into Phil's wet face. Beads of water dripped from the coils in his hair to his temples and continued on down his cheek. His grin was wider than a canyon. "You missed."

"Oops," I grinned. "Sorry about that, I'm almost done."

Once done, we wrapped each other in towels and climbed onto the bed. Phil on his back and me by his side with my arm draped across the broad expanse of his chest. Heat rose off of him in waves. His breathing was rough.

"Hey, Phil."

"Yeah?"

"Are you feeling the effects of that oil we got on our hands?"

He was quiet for a moment. "Yes," he said in a whisper. "It should pass though."

The devil was in me and would not leave me alone. I swung my legs over his hips and sat up. "Or, I can take you for a ride."

My lips found his of their own volition. His free hand found my waist and pulled me closer. We separated after what seemed like an eternity.

"Tanzy, that stuff Sunshine brews is potent. There is a reason she is sought-after."

LOST IN LIBERIA

My motor was revved up high. He was beneath me and rock hard. I rubbed my crotch over his shamelessly. "Oh, yeah, I totally get that reason."

"But will we still want to be together tomorrow, or the day after that? Well after the effect wears off?"

"I guess we will have to see."

It was a struggle to pull my panties off. His briefs slid down and were kicked to the side in record time. Our hands were halfway unstuck but there were some spots that still needed to wait. Pretty much the only position we could use was him on his back and me on top. I was good with that. I was so horny, I was out of my mind. I sheathed him in a slow up-and-down motion. He groaned and moved faster.

We picked up our pace until I was riding him like a cowgirl. My breasts jiggled, our skin slapped, our breaths puffed out in shared grunts. I was wild like never before. We came in a frenzied scream. I saw points of light and floated high above. Phil yelled his release and held me close as we came down from the clouds.

I floated away to sleep in his arms. Not even worried if I would want him tomorrow. The answer was yes.

Later, in the wee hours of the morning, our hands slipped apart. Phil rolled me over, spread my legs wide, and entered me gently, rocking. He made love to me for the next few hours. Dawn came and the trees came alive with the sounds of monkeys, birds, and animals.

"It's time to wake up."

"Has the oil worn off?" I asked sleepily.

"Not quite, but we have to get up and meet Sunshine

on the beach."

Chapter 10

*P*_{hil}

Tanzy slipped away to her room around nine with a promise to meet me in the lobby at eleven. She did not disappoint. She showed up in a hot red dress, a summer hat, and red shoes. She had a large rattan bag thrown over her shoulder. I almost hated to tell her that I rented a scooter and that we were going to ride down to Coco Beach with the wind whipping in our faces and her dress fluttering behind us. My approach to the day was a pair of pressed slacks and a lightweight button-down shirt.

I kissed her red lips like a starving man in the desert. "You look amazing." I meant it with every fiber of my being. She was the tsunami that came along and knocked me over. Before Tanzy, I was going through the motions of life instead of living it.

"Thanks, you look scrumptious too," she said with a sweet smile.

"Are you ready to go?"

"I am and I brought this bag along so we can carry the box. Sort of hide it until we are ready to make the transfer."

I liked that idea and immediately reached for the box. It sloshed a little but settled into her bag. The scooter rental agency was on the far side of the lobby. We picked up the keys and found ourselves standing in front of a little red beach scooter, one of those numbers that tourists rent for short trips. Tanzy settled behind me and I pushed off, heading south.

Finding Sunshine would be a tall order if we had not arranged a meeting place. The route took us off the main road and onto a secondary street that soon took us to a five-star resort. There was one thing about Sunshine, she was not cheap.

"Let me see where she is and I'll come back to get you."

"I don't think you'll have to. There's a woman flagging you down over there."

A woman, also wearing a red summer dress, was waving at us. She had a bag draped over her shoulder that looked suspiciously like Tanzy's.

"Tanzy, is red the color for dresses this season?"

"Apparently."

I pulled to a stop at the valet. A young man barely in his twenties approached with the ticket. His uniform was a bit big on him but he had a bounce to his step and big smile on his face.

"Hiya, we'll only be a few minutes." I'd planned on making a fast drop and spending the rest of the day with Tanzy.

"*Si, Señor*," he said as he took the key.

LOST IN LIBERIA

Sunshine met us at the curb, a rueful smile on her face. Her hair was twisted into a fall of braids that cascaded down her back. "Well, I see you're still alive, Fixer," Sunshine greeted me.

"No thanks to you."

Tanzy gasped. "Rocky?"

"Tanzy? Oh my God, you're here with Fixer?" came Sunshine's reply.

I was so shocked; the dumbest question came out of my mouth. "You two know each other?" Not only did they know each other, Tanzy clearly knew her by her real name, Rocky, which was short for Raquel. Sunshine was her code name. I continued to stare back and forth between the two of them.

"Maybe we should take this inside," Sunshine said.

She led us into an open-air lobby. A small waterfall draped the far wall and trickled into a pool full of koi. On the other side of the lobby down a flight of stairs was a small café. We entered and stopped at a booth tucked in the far corner. Sunshine slipped in and we followed suit.

"So, Philip," she began, neatly dropping the code names. "How did you come to meet my cousin?" And in the blink of an eye, my life became more complicated.

"Uhm...we met at the travel agency..." My answer was too hesitant, Tanzy jumped in.

"You see, I was trying to fly to the country of Liberia in Africa and ended up on Phil's flight to Liberia, Costa Rica instead," she explained.

Sunshine's laugh was the same one I remembered. It was light and fake like she was mildly amused.

SAHARRA K. SANDHU

"Liberia, Costa Rica? Tanzy, if I heard that from anyone else, I would have called out the bullshit card. Coming from you, I actually believe it. This in spite of the fact that you stopped making your own reservations last year. Just because of these kinds of mix-ups."

"Are there no secrets in the family?" Tanzy appeared offended.

"Not where you're concerned. Anyway, what on earth are you doing down here on an operation?"

"This is her first one," I interjected, wanting to defend Tanzy. "She's doing great, by the way."

Sunshine made a very unladylike snort. "How many accidents have you had so far?"

"None," I lied, determined not to give her the satisfaction.

"The day ain't over yet. You still have to get back to your hotel in one piece," came Sunshine's droll reply.

"Well, if you must know, I'm in charge of this mission," Tanzy pointed out.

"I'm sorry, cousin, I find that hard to believe. Who told you that?"

"I did." It was technically my idea anyway. The further this conversation went, the madder I got.

"Don't get your briefs in a bunch, Phil. As first missions go, this one is pretty easy. Just pass over the box and you're done."

"Just one second, Miss I'm-so-important," Tanzy interrupted. "You told me at the last family reunion that you were not with the agency. You were a pharmacist.

LOST IN LIBERIA

The last time I looked, pharmacists don't pass around sex toys."

Sunshine leaned in close. "Not that it's any of your business but when Mama J needs my services, she gives me a call. She pays very well, I might add."

"I fail to see why they would send for a pharmacist from Florida. Don't they have any local ones?"

"Not with my special formula for erectile dysfunction or ED. When CBD creams and other pills won't work, men call me for help. You'd be surprised how important virility is to a man. The agency needed to get one of its technical devices close to one of the ministers who works in the Costa Rican free-trade zone. When the first attempt failed, they arranged for him to find me after they discovered his medical problem. He contacted me and I agreed to come down. Of course, I cut a deal for my unique services with Mama J. The rest was child's play as far as mixing my compound here in the country as I can't bring anything across the border." She patted her bag. "It's all right here and you just need to hand over the package that I will leave behind as a parting gift." She nodded toward Phil. "I needed Fixer here to prep it for me. I assume it's primed and ready to go?"

"Yes, of course," I grated. "Tanzy, pass it to her under the table."

Tanzy reached into her bag and slid it along the bench. Sunshine smoothly slipped it into her bag.

"Grandma must have given all us girls the same bag as a Christmas gift last year," Tanzy observed.

Sunshine hefted it to let the box settle to the bottom

and placed it next to Tanzy's bag. "Yes, she did. She found a good deal on them in the Bahamas and had cousin Carissa ship them north in time for the family Christmas celebration. It's kinda nice, don't you think?"

I was not sure what to think anymore. Sunshine was still the same stiff Sunshine. It was probably why Mama J introduced me to her. She was a mirror of myself. After meeting Tanzy, I realized I didn't need a mirror. I needed someone to complement me.

"So, what happens next? Do you call them to come and get you and take you to your patient?" I asked.

"Pretty much. I like to keep things simple."

"Though, I do think it's ballsy to go into a situation by yourself," I noted.

"Do I hear a hint of concern, Phil?"

"Not one bit."

"Oh, don't be so testy. Greg, my partner on this run, is waiting for me in the lobby. He's going with me. Phil, we really must bury the hatchet, so to speak, and let bygones be bygones. Especially if you're running around Costa Rica with the queen of disaster. You'll need all the good karma you can get."

"That tears it. I'll not sit here and be insulted on my first op by you. I don't care that you're my cousin," Tanzy hissed. She grabbed her bag and stood.

"Well, be mad if you must. I know Phil here is lying about you being in charge. There is no way in hell Mama J would authorize this. Tell her, Phil."

"Is this true?" Tanzy asked me.

LOST IN LIBERIA

The lie was on my lips. The words were there to deny everything. But Tanzy was precious to me and I wanted to be honest, but also didn't want to hurt her. My inner turmoil was thick with emotion. The tick above my eye shuddered into a fast mambo. The war between my conscience and the lie raged preventing me from uttering a sound. In the end, I hesitated a bit too long.

Tanzy's eyes narrowed; her gaze focused on my dancing brow. I'd known her for a couple of days, but in that short time, she'd learned how to read me like a book. "That's it. Don't you ever speak to me again," she yelled, turned and stormed away.

"Tanzy, wait."

Sunshine shook her head in pity. "Let her go. She'll cool down."

"You may think this is fun and games but I don't," I spat.

"She really Tanzied you, didn't she?"

"Don't you say that. Don't you ever say that again," I yelled at her.

Sunshine looked in her bag. Her expression changed from disdain to alarm. "Shit, shit, shit," Sunshine cursed.

"What's the problem?" Not that I really cared.

"That moronic cousin of mine grabbed the wrong bag."

My gaze caught Tanzy's retreating form. She was now leaving the far side of the café. A short stalky man intercepted her. His black suit barely closed over his barrel chest. I spotted the gun in his hand. I had no more words for Sunshine. Tanzy's safety was all that mattered.

I prayed I could intercept them before they reached the elevator.

LOST IN LIBERIA

Chapter 11

*Hello, adventurers, this is your girl Tanzy T from DC.
I just stormed out on my date.
Don't know how you feel about travel drama,
but it sucks the big one!
My suggestion is to beware of bad food,
bad men, and bad elevators.
#lovinlifeandlivinit*

*T*anzy

My heart was broken. I'd only known Phil for such a short time, so why did this hurt so much? I know why because he was the first person I met who seemed to understand me. He built up my confidence instead of tearing it down after every bump in the road. This betrayal hurt. I never wanted to see him again. My vision blurred with unshed tears. I bumped into a few people sitting at the café. My feeble apologies whispered in the wind. One look at my face and they moved out of my way. I stormed out of the exit and ran into a man who was shaped like a brick wall and dressed in a black suit which was quite unusual as most men at the resort were dressed in shorts, flowered shirts, and flip-flops. I felt the gun in my ribs and knew something had gone wrong.

"This way, Sunshine," he said in a heavy accent.

He herded me toward the elevators. *No, not the elevators!*

"Sir, I really can't go in there."

"Shut up and get in." He reached around me and pressed the up button.

"You don't understand. Me and elevators don't jive."

"*Que*? What are you talking about? Just follow my orders." He dug the gun in deeper.

"Ouch, that hurts. Listen to me. Every time I'm near an elevator, it breaks. We must use the steps."

The bell chimed, announcing the arrival of the elevator. The doors slid open and several people exited. They were dressed for the pool or the beach. The smell of suntan lotion wafted in their wake. My legs refused to move.

"*Mueve*! Move, *Señorita*." He pushed me and I stumbled in."

"Sir, I mean it. You need to rethink this whole elevator thing. The stairs are right there." I pointed to the wide staircase that swept up toward the lobby. It was two floors of glorious cardio action. There was time, the doors were only halfway closed. I moved to leave. He grabbed me and pulled me back. The door had only inches to close. At the last second, a hand speared the gap. The door popped back open. Phil stepped in and the doors slid closed behind him.

"What are you doing here?" I raged. "Didn't I tell you to never speak to me again?"

"Sunshine, listen to me."

LOST IN LIBERIA

Why the hell did he call me Sunshine?

"Hey!" The man with the gun waved it in front of both of us. "Shut up and push the button."

Phil turned to comply.

"Not you, her." He pointed his gun at me.

"I tried to warn you." I extended my pointer finger and pressed the starred "L" for the lobby.

With a gentle glide, the elevator began its ascent.

"Haven't you done enough, Phil?" Anger and shame coursed through my veins. I wanted to be a spy so much that I believed him. His dazzling smile and good looks sealed the deal.

"Sweetheart, let me explain." The look on his face was so sincere.

"There is nothing to explain. You built up my hopes and dreams on a lie. A LIE!" I screamed. "I can't believe I was so gullible. And to top it all off, I slept with you."

"That's because you glued us together." He held his hand as proof.

"It was an accident."

Our kidnapper waved his gun at us. "You glued him to you?" His gaze dropped to Phil's crotch and then to me. "That's sick."

"No, it wasn't like that. Besides, I really like her," Phil argued.

I looked away from him unable to stomach another lie. "Will you tell him I'm not speaking to him ever again?" I asked the gunman.

The man's mouth hung open in disbelief. "Will you two stop arguing? This is like watching one of my telenovelas. Except, I'm in it."

"Are you comparing us to a melodrama?" For some odd reason, I was offended.

"Will shooting him make you happy?" He took aim at Phil's head. All the air escaped from my chest. I was mad, but I didn't want him shot dead.

"Listen, maybe we should calm…"

The elevator jerked to a halt, interrupting the argument. The silence that followed was palpable. My heart galloped at an alarming pace.

I glance at Phil, unwilling to move a step. "The elevator has stopped."

"Yep, I see that," came his strained reply.

A high-pitched ringing noise trilled through the space, followed by a muffled voice speaking to us from the control box. He spoke in Spanish.

"What did he say?" I asked.

"Remain calm, help is on the way," Phil translated.

Sweat broke out on the gunman's brow. Tremors took over, which would not have been a problem if the hand holding the gun was more steady.

"Sir, are you okay?"

He shook his head and loosened his tie. "I'm not so good in closed spaces."

"You have got to be kidding me," Phil said. "A claustrophobic kidnaper. What are the odds?"

"Not a good time for this, Phil," I admonished him.

The air got warmer as the minutes passed. The gunman unbuttoned his jacket and lowered his bulk to the floor.

LOST IN LIBERIA

"Look, we may be in here for a while, what's your name?" I asked.

"Ignacio," he answered in between puffs of air.

"Well, Ignacio, let's put up your gun. And I want you to take deeper, and slower breaths."

He nodded and shifted to expose the holster under his left arm. His hand trembled so much it took three tries before the gun slid home. Sweat showered off his brow, his shirt stuck to his chest. I was worried he would have a heart attack right there in front of us.

"Phil, let's show him how to control his breathing. One, two, three, in. One, two, three, out. That's it." I used my calm voice even though I wanted to scream and shout. Ignacio copied our example and settled into a steady breathing pattern. Even still, I felt the need to do more.

"Okay, that's good, Ignacio. Now I'm going to look at the elevator controls and see if there is something I can fix."

I shifted over to get a good look at the panel. There were only three floors. The ground floor where we got on, the first floor, and up on top, the lobby floor. The hotel was designed to cascade down the hill to the beach. So, the lobby was actually the highest point in the property. I pressed the "L," we rose a little, then jerked to a stop.

Ignacio screamed. "No, no, no, don't touch it again," he wailed.

"It's okay, I've been through this before." I looked at Phil. "Do you have a screwdriver? Maybe we can open this thing up and work on it." Phil stared at me as if I were a zombie. He waved for me to move over.

"Step away from the control panel," he whispered.

"I can fix it." I thumped the panel and the elevator jerked, but this time dropped a foot. The lights flickered and dialed down to a weird twilight illuminated by the wan glow of the emergency strobes. "Stop that and come back on," I screamed. "You're scaring us half to death." I stomped my foot in frustration. The floor shuddered. The lights returned to normal.

Ignacio wailed and began to pray. "*Dios Mio, esa chica esta loca. Dejala por favor, Señor.* Stop her!" Ignacio screamed.

"Sunshine, I have the screwdriver but let me do it. I need some room to work. Can you please hold Ignacio's hand and try to calm him down?" I swear he spoke to me like I was a toddler.

"Okay, fine." I moved out of the way and plopped down by Ignacio. "Scoot over," I ordered, crossed my arms, and stuck my tongue out at Phil. I couldn't help it; he made me so angry I could scream. I would have screamed too, but one look at Ignacio's pale face and I changed my mind. No sense in upsetting him more. Besides, Phil was the Fixer, not me, so he probably had a better feel for these types of problems.

Ignacio shifted to the left and I settled against the wall.

"Talk to him," Phil said in a gentle voice.

LOST IN LIBERIA

There was nothing else to do, might as well chat to pass the time. "Hi, what made you go into this line of work?"

"Sunshine!" Phil hissed.

"Why do you keep calling me that?" I demanded.

"Because you're Sunshine," Ignacio added.

Did he mistake me for my cousin?

I turned to Phil for clarification. "What's going on?"

"Check your bag and you'll understand." He had the control plate open and was fiddling with the wires.

I looked in my bag and found the box with the butt plug and another smaller case. Inside the case were three vials of an injectable liquid. *What. The. Hell?*

"Uhm, Phil, this is…"

"Your bag, Sunshine," he finished the sentence. Of course, that was not what I was going to say. It finally filtered into my thick skull that Ignacio thought I was Sunshine and Phil wanted me to go along with the ruse.

Oh boy, Tanzy the terrible struck again. I picked up the wrong bag and was now stuck in an elevator with my would-be abductor and the man I'd just broken up with. This was a triple bad luck whammy.

"Keep talking to Ignacio. He doesn't look too good."

"Hi there, my name is, uhm…Sunshine. Uh…do you have a family?"

His clothes were soaked through and he shook like a leaf. "*Si*, a wife, a son, and two daughters."

"That's nice, what are their ages?"

"My son is *diez*, ten years old. My middle daughter is twelve and my oldest will be fifteen this weekend."

He seemed to relax. His breathing evened out more.

"Are you going to have a... What do they call it? Ahh yes, a *quinceañera*?"

"Si, we have it all planned. It's costing me a fortune, that's why I took this extra job to bring you to the boss."

"You know, I heard those parties cost a bundle. Are you going to Mass before it starts?"

"*Si*, always. *Siempre*. We must give thanks."

"I'm almost there. Keep him talking, Sunshine," Phil added. Wires tumbled out of his hand but he seemed to know what he was doing.

"What are the colors for the party, Ignacio?" I continued.

"She won't say what her dress will be, she wanted it to be a surprise. For the men, we will wear suits with purple vests," he said the last part with a smile. Tears welled; he had a plaintive look. "Are we going to die?" He sniffled.

"Well, Ignacio, this guy right here, Phil, he can fix anything. He should have us out of here in nothing flat."

He wiped his face and straightened his back against the wall a bit. "Thank you, *Señorita*. I'm sorry I was so mean to you. They tell me not to make friends with the people I come to pick up. But you are so nice to me."

"It'll be okay, Ignacio."

"I think I got it," Phil announced.

He pushed the wires back inside the opening, closed the panel, and pressed the "L." The elevator shuddered once. Ignacio and I grabbed each other for support.

LOST IN LIBERIA

"I know this will work." Phil pressed it again. The elevator jerked up, down, then rose smoothly to the next floor. The doors slid open and fresh air breezed in. I did not realize how stuffy it had gotten.

"*Gracias Dios*!" Ignacio warbled. He rolled to his knees before he could get his feet under to stand. Both he and Phil helped me up. We filed out into the lobby amongst stares and applause.

"I'm so sorry, I have to take you to my boss," Ignacio apologized.

"It's okay, big fella. Just lead us on," Phil assured him.

We walked out to the front where three more men waited.

"I sure hope this is a short drive," Phil whispered.

"Hush, I'm still not talking to you," I whispered back.

The men hustled us into the car without a word. Phil and I sat in the back while Ignacio took the passenger seat next to the driver. This was the fate meant for Sunshine. She did not seem concerned when we spoke in the café, but I was scared out of my mind.

Chapter 12

Hello, adventurers, this is your girl Tanzy T from DC.
One of the fun things about travel is getting off the beaten path!
Exploring a rainforest is a perfect activity for you adventure hounds.
Remember to dress in good hiking boots and jeans and lots of bug spray!
As for me, I prefer glamping.
That's traveling by car and chillin.'
Check out the cute dress and shoes.
#lovinlifeandlivinit

*T*anzy

We rode for an hour but it felt like a lifetime. I looked out the window to see if there were any landmarks or road signs I could identify. Something, anything, that I could identify just in case we had to make a run for it. No such luck. Verdant forest rolled by, tree after tree. The road was pitted, and deep ruts ran down the middle. We turned onto a paved highway but after a couple of miles turned back off onto a road that was in worse condition than the first. A mountain loomed in the distance, its peak obscured by clouds. I was hopelessly lost by the time we reached the front gate of a compound. To pass the time, I took a few selfies of myself and posted them.

The driver spoke to the man on guard. He pressed a few buttons and the gate silently slid open. Soon, a two-story home came into view. Each floor had a veranda spanning each side. The car pulled up and a man dressed like a butler came down the steps to open our door.

He bowed in greeting. "Welcome, *Señorita* Sunshine. My name is Juan, *Señor* Loprieto's assistant. It's a pleasure to meet you."

I stepped out of the car and motioned toward Phil. "Thanks, this is my assistant Phil."

"It's nice to meet you as well." Juan shook his hand. "Señor Loprieto will greet you in the front room."

"Nice digs," Phil observed.

We followed Juan up the steps and into the house. Ignacio and the driver stayed behind. The house was built with an open floor plan. Off to the right were the kitchen and dining room. To the left was a sitting room, complete with a cherry red piano. In front of us were floor-to-ceiling windows that led out to a patio with a spectacular view of the valley below.

A man, no more than a couple of inches taller than me, stepped in from a room that looked like a study. He had to be seventy if he was a day. He had a paunch and was mostly bald, but not too bad-looking. He probably was handsome in his day. His suit was immaculate and looked like it cost a zillion dollars.

"*Señor* Loprieto, this is Sunshine and her assistant Phil," Juan announced.

The man had a stern look on his face, like he never smiled. I was not sure if we were supposed to bow, shake hands, or make a run for it. I chose to act like we were old lost friends.

"*Señor* Loprieto, it's so nice to meet you."

"Sunshine, the pleasure is mine." He smiled and held out his hand in greeting. This was comforting. "I've heard about your success and am honored that you were willing to travel down here to meet me."

"You made a request I couldn't refuse and I hope I'll be able to help you."

"Would you like some light refreshments before we start?"

"Why yes, we would," Phil interjected. I was glad he did. My first instinct was to drop off the box and vials and run. At least he saved me from the serious faux pas of not accepting a drink from the host.

They guided us to a beautiful wooden table located on the veranda. The light meal consisted of a choice of beef, poultry, or fish. A smorgasbord board of cheese and wine choices and a salad filled out the spread. Mr. Loprieto had a very different definition of a small meal compared to mine. I was expecting ham sandwiches, chips, and beer.

"I'd like to use your facilities to wash my hands."

"Of course, the bathroom is right around that corner."

Once I finished with my ablutions, I returned and dove in. The food was superb and the company was not too shabby. We chatted about fun things to see in his country, and the general area surrounding the compound.

LOST IN LIBERIA

One of the mountain peaks was an active volcano. Mudslides were a regular occurrence. I learned that the forest had a unique biodiversity. Not much I could use but I listened and assured him I would explore before I returned home. After I ate my meal, we were instructed to meet *Señor* Loprieto in his private study.

We walked across the living room and up a flight of stairs that led to two wooden doors. A picture of the surrounding forest was etched into the wood. Birds flew in the skies, monkeys played in the trees. This was an idealized representation of the compound. It was so different, I had difficulty believing that there was nothing to be worried about and yes, I will admit to having seen way too many spy movies. The people who got trapped in the compound always ended up running for their lives. I hoped our day here would not come down to that.

We found *Señor* Loprieto sitting at the desk. He pointed to the two chairs placed in front. "Please have a seat, my friend," he said in a warm, cheerful voice.

"I'd like to thank you for your hospitality. *Señor* Loprieto," I said. "You're too generous and kind."

"Ignacio and Juan, please step outside and give us a few minutes."

They exited quietly and efficiently, leaving us alone with the *señor*.

"Now, let's start from the top," Loprieto began. He stood up and walked around the desk to stand in front of it.

"Dr. Sunshine, last week we spoke on the phone about my options," he paused waiting for my reply.

I had no choice but to go with the flow and pray I did not make a slip. "Why yes, we did," I said with a bright smile." My insides were turning to jelly.

"So, I decided that I would like to take the injectables."

"Good choice. I'm sure you will be pleased with the results." Sweat gathered at my temples.

"I'm glad you agree. You said you need to examine me before we start?"

"I did?" Butterflies took up residence in my stomach.

"Of course, you did doctor," Phil jumped into the conversation to cover my lapse.

"Very well then," *Señor* Loprieto said and with a flip of his wrists, he neatly unzipped his pants. They slithered to the floor exposing his nether regions. "I'm ready for you to proceed."

There was one thing about the man, he was not embarrassed or shy standing in front of us with his lower half exposed. And why would he be? I was Dr. Sunshine here to fix his…personal parts. The problem was this was not my calling, there had been a terrible mistake and I was two seconds away from a meltdown.

"Uhm, *Señor* Loprieto…"

"Please call me Angel."

"Mr. Angel, may I have a brief minute to discuss the treatment plan with my assistant?" The words tumbled out of my mouth like a waterfall tumbling off a cliff. I needed to change my location and was desperate to change it immediately.

Chapter 13

*P*_{hil}

When we reached the guest room, Tanzy was frantic. She was more than frantic; she was in full panic mode.

"I can't do this, Phil," she said as she paced the floor.

"Yes, you can and you will," I assured her.

"He showed me his dick, Phil."

"I realize that, Tanzy."

"He better not want me to touch it, Phil."

"We'll tell him you don't do that, Tanzy."

She stopped pacing and gazed at me. There was desperation in her gaze. "I don't think you understand."

I wanted to allay her fears. "Tanzy…"

"I. Am. Terrified," she hissed. "You don't get it. I'm Tanzy the terrible, the mistress of mishap, the diva of disaster, the maven of mistakes. I can feel when a calamity is about to strike and right now it's taking aim at that old man's dead dick," she paused; her breath passed her lips in hard puffs. "You saw what happened in the elevator. The way my luck is running today, I'll break his business just by looking at it. Heaven only knows what would happen if I touched it. Look me in the eye and tell me you really want me to come close enough to pump up his peter."

My gaze connected with hers. I did not blink or waver. "Sweetheart, I believe in you. You've been fed a lot of crap from your family yet, the Tanzy I know is more than capable of anything she puts her mind to."

Tears brimmed her eyes. "That is so sweet of you to say. But, I'm pretty sure that now is not the time to test your theory. Our lives are at stake. Did you see all the guns his men carry? If I mess up, he'll have us whacked for wrecking his willy. I can't go near him, Phil."

She had a point but we were in too deep to back out. "Tanzy, be reasonable. You can't break his dick by looking at it. Besides, you're the one who always finds the silver lining, the positive spin. You'll figure something out."

She was not convinced. "There has got to be something else he can do. I mean, why can't he take Viagra?" She was plaintive.

"It apparently is not working for him. When men with his problem show up at Sunshine's door, she is usually their last hope. They've gone through all other options."

"So, what am I supposed to do?"

"Sunshine has three vials in the box. Apparently, she wanted to use them on him and give him a supply to last him a while."

LOST IN LIBERIA

"They're liquid injectables... I'm not going anywhere near his noodle with a needle, Phil. Not for all the gold in Fort Knox. Ye gods, I can see the tragedy unfolding and it hasn't even happened yet."

"Tanzy, calm down."

"I can't calm down. That man is expecting me to perform a miracle and, believe me, it will take a miracle to raise his flag."

To my credit, I kept a straight face. If only to be the calm in the eye of the Tanzy-fueled storm. I pulled the box with the vials and syringes. "You just tell him to take one vial and fill the syringe half full to start with."

"What is this stuff? Where does he put it? Down his pee-pee or somewhere else? Details are important here."

She had a legitimate path of inquiry. My only hope was that I could guide her through it and get her out of here. "It's a compounded concoction that Sunshine created. The patient is supposed to inject it in the vein that runs along the side."

"Is there an option three?"

"No, Tanzy, you have to carefully give him the directions so he can inject himself. Much like diabetics give themselves injections."

"This is a lot different than diabetics injecting themselves."

"Okay, maybe that was not a good analogy."

"I'll say, you'd be closer comparing it to resurrecting the dead after a long hard life." She wagged her finger. "I mean, he's over seventy, for God's sake. Surely, he's done enough fucking to last the rest of his life!"

I turned away to compose myself. We had to get serious if we were going to succeed in this mission. "Tanzy, I understand your frustration. Let's try not to judge him. Realistically, we're not supposed to be here, yet here we are, and we have got to complete this mission. He'll know we are not the real people if we don't get it together."

"So, you're saying it's my bad luck that got us here?"

"What? No. How can it be? Ignacio happened to pick the wrong girl. It's not your fault."

"The wrong girl who happened to have the wrong bag. My family is right. I'm a walking disaster."

The only way I could get through to her was to speak from the heart. I gathered her in my arms. "Now look, I won't have you talking like this. You are the most amazing and talented woman I've ever met. Things always seem to work out with you even if they appear to be going bad at first. You have this outlook on the world that's bigger than life. That's what makes you special, Tanzy."

"I'm not sure if I believe you but…" Our lips met in a short kiss. One that tasted sweet like summer wine. She was my sugar fix and my first instinct was to stay there and linger, but duty called.

We parted with a promise of more to come. Tanzy had a knowing smile. She was thinking again. I could tell. "One more question."

"Yeah?"

"How come you know so much? Did my cousin do this to you?"

LOST IN LIBERIA

Damn, she was good. She already caught me attempting to lie, so I decided to try honesty.

"Yes, she did."

"What? You said she didn't experiment on you."

"It was a few years ago and I had some problems."

"Well, you seemed to have worked them out if last night was any indication of your recovery."

I wasn't sure if that was a compliment, but I would take it as such. "Just explain the process of injecting the serum to him, give him the butt plug as a gift, and let's get out of here."

"Okay," she hesitated.

"Tanzy, you can do this. Sunshine was wrong when she said you were a disaster. I've spent this day with you and you can be a better spy than the lot of them."

"You really mean that?"

"With all my heart."

"Okay, I'm not happy about this and if it wasn't for the mix-up in the bags, Sunshine would be here instead of me."

"You'll find that you are the right person and it was supposed to be you here today."

"Okay. Just stay by my side. This is Sunshine's ministry and I am way out in the deep end of the pool. He better not expect me to test-drive the boner this shot is supposed to give him."

"I certainly hope so," I said a bit too quickly.

"Are you jealous?"

"If you must know, yes."

*****

We stepped back into the room, *Señor* Loprieto was there waiting. "My God, I hope she gets good money for this," Tanzy whispered under her breath.

"She does, about ten thousand when she is stateside, twenty when she travels."

"Say what? Well then, I'm asking for a raise when we get back."

To her credit, Tanzy performed admirably. She opened the case in one smooth motion. "*Señor* Loprieto, this is a vial of medicine specially compounded for you. You must inject it into the vein that runs along your…uhm."

"I know what to do, remember? You described the process in a phone call," he interrupted.

"Yes, of course. Don't forget an hour before you wish to uhm, have sex."

"I'm ready now. My girls are waiting for me." He whipped his peter out and searched for a vein. There were several.

"Which one?" he asked.

Shit, a question I did not cover. But Tanzy rose to the challenge…so to speak.

"Try that large one."

He fumbled around.

Tanzy expelled a puff of air. "No, not that one, the other one." She took a step closer and pointed until he figured it out.

"Yes, that one," she said.

He hesitated. "Maybe you should do the first one."

LOST IN LIBERIA

I pursed my lips, grimacing, and leaned away in anticipation of the Tanzy explosion. She surprised me with cool, calm professional Tanzy.

"Oh no, *Señor*. You have to learn on the first one. You have a month supply and I won't be here to do it for you."

She was smooth, I'll give her that. *Señor* Loprieto glared at her for a few seconds. All the oxygen sucked out of the room for that one moment before it passed and we could breathe. "You're probably right, but it's hard to get in," he said.

Tanzy tsked. "You gotta grab it like you mean it."

He followed her directions. Tanzy mimed the rest of her instructions. "That's it, now pull it taut and hold it like a rod... That's right, now angle that needle in, and bam, you got yourself juiced for the evening."

To my surprise, he was grinning from ear to ear. She pumped up his ego like a cheerleader at a Friday night game. He looked like a kid about to get a lot of candy. The medicine went in, he pulled out the needle and rubbed his dick like he'd missed an old friend. A few minutes later his pants were back around his waist, belt buckled and shirt straightened. He returned to the opposite side of the desk and sunk down into the chair with a satisfied sigh.

Tanzy grabbed the toy out of her bag and set it on the desk. "Uhm, *Señor* Loprieto, here's a gift that comes with the vials."

"Is this one of your patented butt toys?"

"Why yes," she beamed.

"Delightful. I've heard about them and for the money I'm spending, I better see results."

He looked down at his crotch and smiled. "It feels like the medicine is working."

He spoke into a speaker on the desk. "Juan, you may come back in."

"*Si, Señor?*" Juan said upon entering.

"Their cure worked. Now kill them."

LOST IN LIBERIA

Chapter 14

Hello, adventurers, this is your girl Tanzy T from DC.
When it's time to run for your life,
don't hesitate, put those knees to chest and run!
Oh, and one more thing, unplanned hikes through the forest,
plus heels and a red dress equals mud, muck, and wardrobe drama!
#lovinlifeandlivinit

Tanzy

"Now wait just a minute, mister. We fixed your peter. Is that how you repay people?"

I was outraged. How dare he wave his business in front of me and then order my death. Who did he think he was?

"It's nothing personal. I just can't have word get around that I needed help in the sex department," *Señor* Loprieto said.

"Whatever happened to doctor-client privilege? I'm not gonna tell anyone."

"I can't trust you."

He motioned to Juan. "Take them out back."

Juan grabbed me, forcing me toward the door as he held a gun and waved it at Phil. "Let's go, *Señor*," he said. Phil walked ahead of us then onto the steps down to the ground floor of the house. Latin music filled the air. The scent of gardenias floated on a breeze that flowed throughout the house. It really was a lovely home, except for the fact that the owner wanted us dead. I was so mad at this turn of events that I almost missed Ignacio signaling us. I stumbled, diverting Juan's attention. Phil was ready, he pivoted and slammed his fist into Juan's face. He went down hard, out cold.

Ignacio opened the patio door. "This way, you'll find a car over there by the garage."

"Thanks," I said.

The sunny day had turned solemn and gray. The sky opened up, pelting us with hail and rain. Lightning drew a jagged path to the ground. Thunder boomed in the distance. We were soaked in seconds but I dared not stop. My red dress was plastered to my body, the heals were covered in mud. Phil and I dashed over to a jeep. The top cover was off so this was going to be a wet ride but there was no help for it. I jumped in the driver's seat, Phil in the passenger seat. "I don't see the keys."

He reached between me and the steering wheel and pulled wires. He twisted and bent them but nothing happened.

"Come on, Phil, you can do this."

He spared a quick glance my way and began anew. He reached under again, twisted something else, and the car started. Phil settled into his seat, I put it in gear and aimed for the guard gate at the end of the drive. I rammed into the gate, breaking it in two, turned right, and sped away. Behind us, another jeep followed, it was Juan and Ignacio in hot pursuit.

The road was muddy and wet. The ruts now hidden holes in the water-logged earth. I was not sure which way we were headed but any place else was better than where we were. A hairpin turn appeared ahead, braking seemed imperative but they were right on my bumper.

"Tanzy." Phil's voice rose in alarm.

I did not brake.

"Tanzy!" Phil yelled.

At the last minute, I made the turn and continued up the hill.

"I'm pretty sure we need to go downhill," he pointed out. He hastily buckled his seat belt. His hands were wrapped around the side strap. He held on to the dash. His eyes were wild.

"Look, I got this." I took another turn. Then wham, we were caught in a torrent of mud and water. "It's a mudslide!" I yelled.

The jeep made a long, lazy spin in the muck, tilted, and went over the side of the hill.

Chapter 15

*P*_{hil}

The descent was terrible. The jeep rode the river of mud like a bucking bronco. Debris floated around us, some spilled over into the open cabin. It was cold and wet. Somehow, we managed not to tumble or flip over. I grabbed Tanzy to shield her but lost my grip when we came to a halt. She slid from my grasp and was swept over the door and out into a field. I jumped in after her, frantic that I would lose her.

"Tanzy!" I yelled.

"Phil," came her weak reply.

I spotted red cloth draped over a log. My legs could not move fast enough to reach her side. She was half covered in debris but still alive. Her hair was caked in mud, the dress torn, her face covered in streaks of dirt.

"Can you move?"

"I'm good, just get me out."

We survived by some miracle. Only Tanzy could drive us over a cliff and we live to tell the tale. I was never so happy to see someone in my life. I swooped her up into my arms, kissing every inch of her dirt-stained face. "Don't scare me like that."

"Phil…"

"No, I mean it. Until you came along, I was afraid to live, to feel. You said you were terrified, but I'm always terrified.

"What are you talking about?"

"I'm terrified of being exposed as a phony. I've built this persona as the Fixer, but what if I can't fix that next job? What if I fail and people die?"

As always, she saw straight to the heart of the matter. "Did someone die, Phil?"

It was still hard for me to describe the day my world blew up. I could do it in bite-size chunks, one word, one syllable at a time. "I was sent to a small city in Eastern Europe to help Sunshine. The op was going smoothy until I needed to jump-start a car. You see, it's the simple jobs that bite you. There was an important diplomat and his son inside. I got in and got the car started, but there was a bomb. By the time I realized it was there…it was too late."

"Oh my God. That must have been terrible."

"Sunshine chose to pull me out instead of the diplomat and his son. She'd gotten me out but the blast radius sent me flying. I would not have survived if we weren't so close to the sea and I landed in the water."

"You felt she should have taken them?"

"I was expendable."

"Don't you ever say that. Do you hear me? You are not ever expendable. My cousin understood that too," she yelled.

"You may be right but it didn't keep me from being an ass to her and refusing to see or speak to her. That's why Mama J waited until the last minute to tell me who we were meeting." I looked up at the sky, the clouds were clearing and the sun was lower. "Let's get going. The sun is going down and we'll be losing the light soon."

We stumbled through the muck until we found solid ground.

"Phil, wait." She pulled until I stopped. Her arms wrapped around me. They were warm, so warm. "This must have been a lonely existence for you."

"You have no idea. Then you came along like a bolt of lightning and zapped me back into the world of the living. Watching you these last few days was a revelation. You always manage to keep going no matter the bullshit that gets slung your way. You showed me what life would be like with a partner, a friend, a lover. When you said never to speak to you again, I thought my life was over. And just now, when you were swept away, my world tilted upside down. I knew I couldn't live without you."

Tears filled her eyes. "Damn you, Phil, how can I stay mad at you when you say things like that?"

"Please forgive me and promise not to drive over a cliff anymore."

She buried her head in my chest and sobbed. This is what I loved about her. She felt so deeply and was not afraid to show her emotions. "You're forgiven. I'm not so sure I can keep the promise about my driving."

We walked for an hour through a rain-drenched forest. Wet leaves made the footing treacherous, monkeys chittered in the trees above us. Insects attacked exposed skin. The heavens pelted us with thick droplets of water. Juan and Ignacio were far behind and presumably still looking for us. We trudged on in silence until I spotted a familiar plant on the forest floor.

"Phil, what are you doing?" Tanzy asked.

She stopped beside me as I crouched down to look at the plant. "This plant is a crucial ingredient to Sunshine's special formula. It's hard to find outside of its natural environment and when anyone in her circle comes across it, she asks us to harvest it for her."

She put her hands on her hips and pursed her lips. "You've done this before. How else would you know what to spot and where to look."

She had me there and I could not deny it. "Yes, I came here once before. I remembered the plant from that visit."

It was a bush with broad green leaves and delicate flowers. It resembled a collard green, only the leaf was darker verdigris and smaller. We'd somehow stumbled across a large patch of the plant. I was careful to harvest the mature one and take a few stems from each. The process was fairly simple, layer the leaves on top of each other and after about ten, roll them into a bundle. As we were going to have to walk out of the jungle, I was limited as to how much I could carry. Sunshine would have to return for more.

"Tanzy, can you figure out the GPS coordinates of our location?"

"Sure, but why?"

"So, I can pass it on to Sunshine just in case she wants to come find this area herself."

"I'm so confused. You won't talk to her but you're willing to help?"

"I guess, it's the fixer in me. No matter how sour our personal relationship was, I have to admit that she is good at what she does. And she does help a lot of people with the compounds she makes." That was the best way I could explain it. I made ten small bundles and stacked them. "Do you mind if they go in your bag?"

"No, I don't mind. She's my cousin so I'm sorta obligated to help. Even if she's a witch."

She opened her bag for me to put the bundles inside. I lost my footing, slipped, and fell against a bush while holding the last bunch. The bush had little yellow flowers and stems with thorns that looked fairly lethal.

"Are you okay? What did you just slip on?" Tanzy asked.

"A bush. It's nothing…"

A tingling sensation ran up my leg. "I think this is the kind that may give you partial paralysis, but I'm not sure."

We were surrounded by a lot of jungle. Trees, hundreds of feet tall, loomed above us. Wild flora and fauna grew in the spaces between. This part of Costa Rica was beautiful yet no place to be when the sun went down. We continued our descent, making a path through brush and trees. The scent of rich loam and fauna filled the air.

"We should have walked far enough. Can you get a signal?" I asked.

Tanzy pulled out her phone. "I'm not sure." She waited for the map to load. "Oddly enough, I do have a few bars and am able to pull up a map. There is a highway about a mile from here. We can walk out and hopefully hitch our way back."

We were almost to the highway when numbness crept up my right leg. "Tanzy, can you look at this for me?"

Carefully she rolled up my pant leg. A barb from the plant was embedded in my skin.

"Oh no, Phil. Can we remove it?"

"Can we? Yes. Should we? No."

"Is this one of those things where we pee on it and it slides out on its own?"

The image of Tanzy peeing on my leg popped up in my brain. What worried me more was that I was actually considering it before common sense kicked in. "Let's get to the road. Maybe we can get a ride to a doctor."

In the end, Tanzy helped me stay upright the last few feet to the road. We were in luck. It was Highway 1, the Pan-American Highway that ran from Mexico to the tip of South America. There was some traffic but no one stopped.

"We might as well start walking."

"Which way?"

Tanzy looked at the map on her phone and pointed to the right. "This way."

We struggled to walk the side of the road for about a half hour when a car stopped. It was Ignacio.

"Get in," came his order.

We stared at him for a moment.

"It's okay, I'm here to help."

We both slid into the back seat and closed the door.

"How did you know where we were?"

"The boss put a description out on you. You two stick out like the twin peaks of the mountain over there. You look like hell, by the way. You're lucky one of my friends spotted you first."

He pulled into the road and after a few seconds, he slowed, waited for an oncoming car to pass, and swung around to head in the other direction. Tanzy and I were both alarmed by this sudden change.

"You're taking us back?" she squeaked.

"No, you guys must really be lost or at least bad at directions. You were heading toward the compound, not away. Another mile and you would have run into the road leading to the gate. You two did me a solid back at the elevator. I'm returning you to Coco Beach and your scooter. From there, you're on your own."

*****

Ignacio stopped by a clinic to have the barb removed. The doc gave me an antihistamine and some pain meds, all the while assuring us that my reaction was mild and I would get the feeling back in a few hours.

Ignacio was true to his word and dropped us off at Sunshine's hotel where we left the scooter. The rain was gone, yet the road was still wet. The sky was blue and a cool breeze blew in from the sea.

Tanzy gave him a big hug. "My best to your wife and kids. Have fun at the *quinceañera*," she said.

"I will, *Señorita*."

"She's right. We really appreciate this and hope you don't get in trouble."

"It's all good. The boss calmed down and he has gone halfway through his harem, which is what he wanted. He really liked the toy and says he's going to take it back to city with him. That said, if I were you, I'd leave the area just in case some of his other guys spot you."

Ignacio got back in his car, waved goodbye, and pulled away.

"At least we know that butt plug will end up at his home in the capital," I observed.

"Then our mission was a success," she said with a relieved smile.

There was one last thing to do. I pulled out my phone and called Sunshine.

A familiar voice answered. I realized the sound of her voice no longer made my heart race or my eye jump. "Hey, Fixer, were are you?" she asked.

"We're in front of your hotel."

"You two made it back? I just knew you were a

goner." At least she sounded relieved. "I feared the worst when I saw the man hustle you into the elevator and later into the car."

"I'm glad you were worried about us. Hey, listen, we have your bag. It's full of…produce from the forest. Come down and get it."

Less than two minutes later, Sunshine appeared holding Tanzy's bag. "You two successfully made the drop and gave *Señor* Loprieto the meds?"

"Yes, we did," Tanzy beamed.

"You managed to pull off an important mission. Good on ya. The information we'll receive once the fob remotely taps into their system will be valuable."

I passed her bag over and she gave us Tanzy's.

Sunshine took a quick peek at the contents and gave us a big, approving smile. "Thanks, Fixer…and you too, cousin. I owe you one."

"Thanks, cuz. That means a lot to me."

"Hey, I know I was hard on you. I didn't realize how difficult it must be to deal with family members like us."

"That's true. But it's all good." Tanzy was amazingly charitable about the whole thing. I guess when it comes to family it's best to forgive.

"I'll put in a good word with Mama J. Oh, by the way, I placed a few items in your bag for you."

I hefted Tanzy's bag and sure enough, it was much heavier than before. Sunshine waved and disappeared into the cool recesses of the hotel.

Tanzy helped me swing my useless leg over the seat. She placed her bag in my lap and sat in front. There was not much I could do but let her drive, hang on tight, and pray. I learned several things from this misadventure. The first was to double-check Tanzy's map. The second was never let her drive. The third was to see the first. Yet, here I was breaking all the rules.

"Do you know the way?" I asked.

"Yeah, we go straight ahead, stay on this street, and it should take us right to the hotel..." She paused, turned around, and gave me one of her sweet kisses. "But I'm probably wrong and will get us lost."

I relished her kiss and hated to part. "Woman, haven't you figured it out yet? I love you and don't care what direction you go. Wherever it is, even if it's lost, I'll be right there by your side lost with you."

"Yes!" Tanzy squealed as she wrapped her arms around me, tears running down her mud-stained face.

"Phil, I love you too..." Tanzy shifted too far, moving us outside the center of gravity of the scooter. It tilted precariously to the right. The same side as my dead leg that was unable to brace us.

"Oh no," she said and quickly shifted her weight around. It was a bit too late and the scooter fell over with me on it, adding a few more scrapes to my leg and one more rip in my pants.

A burly tourist dressed in shorts and smelling of coconut sunscreen came to our rescue. He was waiting with his wife for the valet to bring around their scooter and saw the whole thing. He helped right us but stopped short of dusting me off. I was a hot, muddy mess after all.

"Thank you so much," Tanzy said. She turned on the ignition and, miracle of miracles, the scooter started up with a purr. She looked both ways at the traffic yet still did not see the approaching car. It narrowly missed us and passed us by inches with its horn blaring. My eye did not twitch. I guess Sunshine was right. I'd been thoroughly Tanzied and loved every bit of it.

"Uhm, sweetheart." I tapped her shoulder as we sped down the road.

"Yes?"

"The hotel is in the other direction."

"Really? Well, damn."

She swung around in front of another car and sped off this time in the direction of the Bosque.

LOST IN LIBERIA

Chapter 16

Hello, adventurers, this is your girl Tanzy T from DC.
Your girl took a day trip that tested her to the limits.
She made up with her boo and survived a trek through the forest.
Doesn't get any better than that.
#lovinlifeandlivinit

*T*anzy

An hour later, the hotel came into view. Phil's leg was much better and he was able to climb off the bike unaided. He walked with a limp but was otherwise all right. We were both a muddied mess, clothes torn, and stained brown from the trek through the woods. My dress was a complete loss, Phil's slacks and top were full of rips and tears. The cat dragged in better-looking prey than us. We were quite the pair and giggled like kids having fun in the park. The front lobby of Hotel Bosque was as lovely, cool, and serene as ever. We left a trail of caked dirt with every step we took. The day was done and we'd managed to survive. Not shabby for my first-ever assignment.

The manager at the front desk spotted us and waved.

"Oh no, here she comes. What do we say?" I asked.

"The truth," Phil began. "We took a couple's trip up the mountain and slipped in the mud."

"*Dios Mio*. What happened to my lovebirds?" Maria asked. She backed away from us when she got a good look. We must've been pretty bad. You couldn't tell from our behavior. We were very giggly, more from relief than anything else. Phil managed to stand a little taller, sort of presenting a better impression. His leg still drooped but there was no help for that.

"*Hola*, Maria, we had a wonderful time exploring the Guanacaste. The zip-lining and hiking were just a bit muddy though." I embellished the story a bit.

"Yes, we did have heavy rainfall this afternoon and the mountain is prone to mudslides." She side-eyed us with a frown. Can't say I blamed her.

"It was a great adventure for our last day," Phil added.

"You'll be checking out tomorrow?"

"Yes, we will," I assured her. There was no way we were staying a day longer. Not with Ignacio's' warning echoing in my head. "See you later."

I led Phil to the elevators.

"You going to try your luck with the 'vator?" He looked shocked.

After my day with Phil, I was willing to try anything. As it turned out, he showed me that my luck did not define me it enhanced me. He said, I always found the silver lining in a situation, but he showed me how to conquer my fears and live my truth. "Phil, when I'm with you, I can tackle the world and nothing seems impossible. So, let's give it a shot."

"That's my girl," he said.

"This is why I love you. You always believed in me no matter what anyone else said about me. That's your superpower." I gave his mud-caked body a critical inspection. "Besides, I don't think I can drag you up the steps."

"Fair enough," he agreed.

The elevator arrived and with a small amount of trepidation, we stepped in. We rose, passing the first floor successfully, then the second—still no hitch. We arrived at the third floor and stepped out without incident.

Phil pulled me into his arms, and our lips met. The kiss made my head swim. "You see, we can beat luck," he announced.

He was right but it was best not to tempt fate. "Shhhh, don't say that too loud," I joked.

"Just so you know, you're the one I want to spend the rest of my life with," he said after another long kiss.

I was so happy, my legs moved to the beat of my happy dance. Two steps right, then left, forward, back, and spin. This man right here knew how to twirl my heart around and hold it close. I was hooked on tall, dark, and Phil for a reason. To be truthful, he had me from the moment I spilled coffee on him and it had nothing to do with luck but everything to do with Phil.

"Through thick and thin? Good luck and bad?" I asked.

Phil nodded. "All of it and everything, my love."

*****

Phil

I meant every word. Tanzy blasted her way into my orderly world like a comet from space, screaming in from the right and sliding to a photo finish with a loud boom. She was the piece that was missing in my life.

We made it to my room and the first order of business was to wash away the forest. It felt like the mud seeped into every crease I owned. "Let's take a shower."

"Together?" she asked.

"But of course."

Tanzy plopped her bag on the table. It landed with a dull thump. "What on earth did Sunshine put in here?"

"Let's see."

Three boxes tumbled out. Images of the contents were artfully drawn on the covers. "I think these are…"

"Sex toys? She gave us sex toys as a gift?" Tanzy asked.

"I believe she did." Two of the boxes held butt plugs, the other held a dildo. A note was taped to the front that said: *Open me, I'm a surprise.*

"I believe this is Sunshine's way of apologizing."

"We can check this out later. I'm too pooped to think right now," Tanzy said.

"I agree. I'll start the water…" But then the phone rang.

LOST IN LIBERIA

"What now?" Tanzy asked.

"It's Mama J calling."

I answered. It was always best to get these calls out of the way so I could have the rest of my time to myself.

"Yes, ma'am," I answered. "How can I help you?" I put the phone on speaker.

"I just got off the phone with Sunshine," she began. "It seems the mission was a success."

"Thanks," we both said in unison.

"Tanzy, are you still interested in working with the agency?"

Tanzy's voice caught in her throat. "Yes!" she screamed.

"Understand that we'll start off slow with easy assignments."

"Okay, but shouldn't I have a code name?" Tanzy asked.

"I was thinking maybe Shadow," I answered. I'd been giving her code name a lot of thought and Shadow seemed to fit the bill.

"I like it. It suits me well. I slide in and slide out as quiet as a mouse." She zigzagged across the floor.

"Nice, Philip. But first, Tanzy, I owe you a trip to Liberia…the country," Mama J said.

"I get to go to Africa?"

"You leave first thing tomorrow morning."

"Thank you, Mama J, I won't disappoint you."

"I'll hold you to that, Tanzy. Have a good trip." Mama J hung up.

"Now to that shower, Ms. James."

SAHARRA K. SANDHU

LOST IN LIBERIA

Chapter 17

Hello, adventurers, this is your girl Tanzy T from DC.
It's time to head home and find another adventure.
One more night, one more sunset, one more shower in this
fabulous bathroom. Saying adios to Costa Rica!
#lovinlifeandlivinit

*P*_{hil}

The rainfall showerhead cascaded warm water over us. It wasn't quite like the real rainfall we found ourselves in earlier but it worked as advertised. Mud sluiced off of our entwined bodies, our clothes having been peeled off and discarded in the trash the moment we entered the bathroom. The jasmine shower gel made mounds of soap suds. We scrubbed, kissed, and scrubbed some more. My lips found hers but I continued on around her chin to the sensitive spot behind her ear. She rubbed her body against mine. We were skin to skin, heart to heart, soul to soul. Her hands rubbed circles around the small of my back. I clutched her hips and pulled her tight.

Tanzy wrapped her leg around my thigh to lift herself higher. I was rock hard, ready, and out of my mind wanting her. Water slid down our skin, landing in splatters and collecting in the tray of the shower.

"Phil?"

"Yeah?"

"Why does it feel like we are standing in a tub of water?"

I came up for air long enough to spare a glance down at our feet. The water was an interesting soapy pale brown, it was also ankle-deep. "Shit, it's backed up."

We jumped apart. Tanzy stared. "Gee, Phil, this usually happens to me with the toilet. We flooded the shower. This is a first for me." Her study of the stall was almost clinical. "I think we clogged the drain with all that mud we carried on ourselves. Dayam, that was one hell of a lot of mud."

The shower knob on the wall resisted my attempts to turn. Water continued to fall from above, and the level rose in the pan. "If we don't stop the shower, it will flood the bathroom," Tanzy warned.

I shook the knob and it came off in my hand. The water continued to flow. "Wrap yourself in a towel. I'll call the front desk."

By the time maintenance arrived, we were sloshing through a shallow pool. A small tsunami rolled out into the hallway when I opened the door. Sudsy water washed over the guy's boots. He cast a baleful eye at my toweled body, then leaned over to look past me toward Tanzy. She tightened the towel around her bosom, straightened, and held her chin high.

LOST IN LIBERIA

His expression was amused yet slightly annoyed. "*Señor*, I believe you have a problem," he observed.

I gave him my best poker face. "I believe we do."

He sloshed by me, angling toward the bathroom door. His boots slipped but he managed to remain upright, the soap made for a treacherous walk across the tiled floor. He peered into the bathroom and muttered something under his breath about Americans. With a heavy sigh, he entered and went to work.

Tanzy sauntered over. She adjusted the towel higher on her chest and dangled a room key between her fingers. "Hey, Phil, remember, I still have my room."

I grinned. All we really had to do was collect my suitcase, her bag full of toys, and tiptoe upstairs.

"Lead the way, my dear."

*****

Tanzy

I would love to say that we jumped each other's bones as soon as we made it to my room, but that would not completely be the truth. We were, at the core, two geeks who'd just been given toys. Yes, they were sex toys, but toys nonetheless. We cuddled up on the bed, jettisoned the boxes, and tried to turn them on. We were an hour into working out the bugs. Apparently, Sunshine got a deal from some manufacturer in Korea. The instructions were in four languages: Korean, Chinese, Vietnamese, and Tagalong. Needless to say, we didn't read any of those languages. We decided to decipher the pictures instead.

"Are you sure about this?" I asked Phil.

He pointed to the caption on the page. "Yeah, it said download this app. We now have the app on our phones…"

"So, we set up the Bluetooth to talk with them."

"Yep, that's it."

"Then we control them with our phones?"

"Uh-huh."

I held up my toy. It was bedazzled with blue rhinestones. White stones adorned the middle in the shape of a cursive *T*. Phil's was identical to mine except his had a cursive *P*. "Do I really want to know how or why my cousin runs down to another country carrying butt plugs with our initials on them?"

Phil rolled his eyes but kept silent.

"Oh, go on and tell me. I'll get it out of you anyway."

"Okay, you twisted my arm. She's a frustrated artist. She carries the crystals and glue when she travels, and in her spare time, she does this. Think of this as a fancy way to say she was sorry for treating you so badly."

Wow, I was not expecting that answer. "I thought you were going to regale me with a story of how she had issues and had to make a choice between decorating sex toys or doing hard drugs."

He laughed. "No, nothing like that."

"You think you know someone, then bam, something odd comes out of left field. Does she sell them?"

LOST IN LIBERIA

"She makes quite a bundle in the anniversary boxes she puts out on her website."

"I've heard enough. Let's fire these babies up before I back out." I thought better of that description. "I mean, change my mind."

We held our phones side by side and opened the app. As apps go, this one was pretty straightforward. A couple of taps later the plugs were vibrating.

"Well, I'll be damned. They work," I said.

"I'll put yours in you and you do mine."

"What do we do first?"

"Get out of the bed and lean over the end."

We got into position.

"Now we oil them up and put a little oil in the intended destination."

"You mean asshole?"

Phil doubled over and could say no more. His laugh was infectious and I joined him. I lubed up his toy and gently massaged it into place. He groaned and smiled.

"Now it's your turn."

This would be my first time. I was a virgin, so to speak, and froze, not sure what to do.

"Tanzy, relax. It's good and oily and so are you. We can wait if you want."

"Nope, I'm good." With that, I bent over, spread my cheeks, and held my breath.

"You have to breathe."

I took a deep breath and he entered my backside. The passage was tight but with a little massaging back and forth, he pushed past the resistance, and the butt plug was in. I felt the vibrations down to my bones.

"Wow," was all I could utter.

Phil pulled me into the middle of the bed, enfolding me with his arms. "How do you feel? I don't want you to be uncomfortable."

"I'm good but a little breathless." It felt like a few honey bees took up residence in the lower half of my body. Not unpleasant and kind of thrilling.

"Do you want to play with the controls?"

He did not have to ask me twice. "Hand me my phone." The app had a few settings and I pushed the dial to two. Nothing happened, so I pushed it to five. "Damn thing is not working.

Phil jumped. "Whoa. Dial it back!"

"What's wrong?"

He grabbed his phone and dialed it to five. What felt like bees a few seconds ago turned into a hive. I went from zero to 'oh honey, help me' in nothing flat. "Our phones crossed the Bluetooth signals. Yours controls mine and mine controls yours."

I dialed down the gain, so did Phil. We held each other and laughed. Then passion took over. Soon, he was deep inside of me, rocking to a tempo set up by the vibrator. The bed was not placed firmly against the wall. The small gap allowed it to rock back and forth with us. The thrusts grew deeper and harder, and the bed smacked the wall with a steady *thump, thump, thump*.

The vibration set up by both our plugs made us crazy. We moaned, screamed, and shouted until we peaked together, stiffened, and yelled out our release. Nothing prepared me for the stars that floated in my head.

We were sweaty, tired, and limp. The vibrators hummed. Phil released me and we separated with a satisfied moan.

"I guess we should turn them off," Phil said.

"Where are the phones?" I'd lost track of them. "They must be somewhere here in the bed."

Phil lifted his and searched the front of the bed. "I see them."

He stretched his arm to reach them. I wriggled against the glory of his abs, eliciting a rumbled laugh from his chest. His chuckle added to the good vibrations for sure.

"Don't make me laugh, Tanzy. They're close to edge and I don't want to…"

I heard a thump, then another thump.

"Philip, what was that?"

"Oh, it's Philip now?"

"It is when it sounds like the only way to turn these things off has fallen off the bed."

"What are you going to call me when I tell you they've slipped through the space at the head of the bed and we'll have to move it completely away from the wall to retrieve them?"

I could not help it. The laughter came from my toes, moved through my body, and erupted from my mouth into rolling giggles. "Please tell me you're joking," I said between the giggles.

Phil had tears in his eyes, he laughed so hard. "No,

I'm not joking."

"Do you think we should call the maintenance guy from your room?" I was laughing so hard my side ached.

"To find the phones or pull the plugs out our asses?" He was half off the side with laughter.

We snorted and laughed for several minutes. It took us a while to compose ourselves.

"Phil, I guess this is the Tanzy effect."

"No, this was definitely all my fault. In case you haven't noticed, my luck is not much better than yours. My family used to call it the Phil factor," he said a bit ruefully.

He pulled me into the sweetest embrace a girl could ever have. He kissed me silly erasing what little sense I had left. "Let's call it even. You've been Tanzied and I've been Philled."

Fresh laughter bubbled up from his chest. "Guess what? You've been *Philled* in more ways than one."

He wrapped the sheets around us and showered me with kisses. We were skin to skin, legs entwined, hips bumping, and plugs buzzing as we twisted and turned, getting hopelessly tangled, until we tumbled off the bed. We eventually retrieved the phones and pulled the plugs but not without a lot of noise and fun.

LOST IN LIBERIA

Chapter 18

Hello, adventurers, this is your girl Tanzy T from DC.
I'm heading to Africa for real this time.
All thanks to Mama's Travel Agency.
Call her if ya just gotta go!
#lovinlifeandlivinit

*T*anzy

Our flight landed at JFK Airport ahead of schedule. The plan was to transfer in New York for the next leg of the trip to Liberia. I posted the blog as soon as I turned on my phone and was sure to give Mama J and her travel agency some props. She always insisted on a review. This trip did not start out as planned but it ended well. As for the blog, I got almost twenty thousand followers and great feedback.

Phil and I were off the plane and at baggage in short order. My bag came off the belt in fairly good condition for once. However, Phil's was missing.

"Okay, where's my bag?" he asked

The belt stopped and people left with their belongings. After a few minutes, a claxon rang then it began to move. A lone bag slid out of the slot. It'd been opened and closed with a belt around its center. Socks and shirts hung out the gaps at its sides.

"Look at the state of your bag. This happens to you too I see."

"All too often, my dear…all too often."

Phil hefted the remains of his luggage, placed it on the tiled floor, and extended the handle. He did not look surprised or overly concerned. Instead, he shook his head and rolled his eyes. I recognized that reaction, I'd had my fair share of the same experience.

"Look on the bright side. At least the wheels work and you can roll it," I pointed out.

"That's what I love about you. There's always a bright side," he said with a grin.

We transferred to the international terminal after a quick stop at an over-the-top expensive luggage shop to replace Phil's busted bag. Our tickets were for first class and except for Phil's bag, we made it this far without any hitches.

We were soon airborne and on our way. About two hours into the flight the pilot came on with an announcement.

"Good evening, everyone. We have an emergency and will have to divert the flight to Lajes Airport in the Azores. Please bear with us and we will get you on the ground and transferred to your destination as soon as possible."

I had not been on a diverted flight in a long time. We were going to land at Lajes instead of Liberia. I half wondered what it would take to get me to the right place.

LOST IN LIBERIA

"Phil, wake up." I nudged him. He slumbered beside me with a sleeping mask over his eyes. He no longer wore his dark slacks with a matching button-down shirt. His new wardrobe centered around light tan linen with tan dockers. Very cool, less fussy.

"What?" came his mumbled reply. He lifted the end of the mask and squinted my way.

"They're diverting the flight."

"Where to?"

"A place called Lajes."

"Lajes?"

"Yep, that's what he said. Where is it?"

He chuckled and covered his eyes with the mask once more. "It's a city on an island in the middle of the Atlantic. Belongs to Portugal, as I recall… You'll like it."

He snuggled under the blanket and went back to sleep.

Hello, adventurers, this is your girl Tanzy T from DC.
Scratch the Africa post.
Heading to Portugal.
Can't wait to see what trouble I can get into there!
#lovinlifeandlivinit

The End
Lost in Liberia

SAHARRA K. SANDHU

**Be sure to check out *The Vagabond Series*
A collection of standalone travel romances written by
various authors you love!**

Cruisin' to Cozumel by Amy Stephens
Jamaican Me Crazy Mon by Ireland Lorelei
Beached in Bali by Erin Brockus
Belize Bliss by C.L. Collier
Innocent in Istanbul by Heather E Andrews
Adventures In Honeymooning by Barb Shuler & KA Graham
Delayed in Venice by Margot Swan
Loving London by Tina Gallagher
Lost in Liberia by Saharra K. Sandhu
Moonlight in Montreal by Tracy Broemmer
Almost in Amalfi by Leigh Adams
Flirting in Fiji by A.M. Roark
The Singapore Stunt by Mel Walker
Delayed in Zurich by Margot Swan
Under Construction in Bora Bora by Jacie Lennon
Mai Tais and Goodbyes by J.A. Wynters
Delayed in Cape Town by Margot Swan
Broken Down in Ballyclare by Tina Gallagher
Finding True North by E.A. Pierce
A Polar Pursuit by S.E. Rose
Passion in Paris by C.L. Collier
Nights in Nepal by Tarrah Anders

Visit The Vagabond Series website
Join the series' Facebook readers' group
Follow the series' Facebook page
Visit the Vagabond Series Amazon Page

Also By Saharra K. Sandhu

The Mama's Travel Agency Novels

Mama's Travel Agency is a series full of romance and adventure. Based in Washington DC, Mama J, the travel agency's proprietor, will send her unsuspecting couples on romantic trips to exotic locales. These contemporary romantic comedies are penned for the reader who wants something sassy, funny, and full of unexpected twists. Check out Mama's Travel Agency, call her if ya just gotta go!

Spice Island
(Book 1 of the Mama's Travel Agency Novels)

Queisha's Cove
(Book 2 of the Mama's Travel Agency Novels)

Also from
SAHARRA K. SANDHU
Daughter of the Missing
(Book 1 of the Gaiian series)

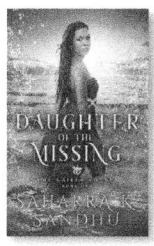

What would you do if you were swept out to sea
...without a boat?

Astronaut Sarai Mathews knows the end is near when a giant wave rolls in and pulls her from the beach. But something strange happens she doesn't die. Instead, she lives and breathes...underwater. While in the depths, she meets a man named Jon Luc. According to him, they're both *Gaiians*, a race of beings who are equal parts human and earth spirit. She is a descendant of their missing queen who was lost to slavery. Could any of this be true? Is he real and not just someone she dreamt up during the chaotic moments in the water? Find out when you read Saharra K Sandhu's debut novel, *Daughter of the Missing*.

Daughter Of The Missing **is available at Amazon.com**
E-book   Paperback

FIRE IN ICE
(Book 2 of the Gaiian series)

Only ice can contain the fire that burns within…

Dr. Martel Da Mar is on a mission to solve the mystery surrounding the disappearance of a glacial lake located high in the Patagonia ice fields of Argentina. An unknown heat source has melted the lake and the runoff of the water threatens towns and villages below. As the leading scientist in glacial hydrology, he knows this can't be dismissed as global warming. He soon discovers there is something in one of the remaining blocks of ice that radiates an unusual type of heat signature. If they could harness the power, it would be a great source of energy for civilization. There is only one problem; this source of energy is coming from the dragon. It is about to wake…and it is not alone.

Fire In Ice, available at Amazon.com

ABOUT THE AUTHOR

Saharra K. Sandhu is an award-winning author and lover of all things involving chocolate. She pens fast-paced paranormal romance and romantic comedies full of adventure, and humor. Her misadventures have taken her from the Caribbean to South America and across the Pacific to New Zealand and beyond. Along the way, she has collected Afro-Caribbean stories and folklore to fuel the imagination that generates her books. There are two series, the paranormal Daughter of the Missing series and the contemporary Mama's Travel Agency series. She aims to give you a good chuckle or even an outright belly laugh with some of the situations her characters find themselves. Her stories have twists and turns designed to keep readers guessing till the end. Be prepared to travel to exotic locals or even out of this world. Her novel, Spice Island, a multi-cultural romantic suspense, won the 2019 Emma Award for Contemporary Fiction. The sequel, Queisha's Cove, won the Romance Slam Jam 2022 Emma Award for Best Romantic Comedy. To learn more and stay on top of the latest shenanigans, please visit her website, and sign up for her newsletter at www.saharraksandhu.com.
Happy writing, happy reading.

Newsletter   *Website*

LOST IN LIBERIA

Connect with Saharra K. Sandhu

You can keep up with the adventures of Saharra via her website, and social media pages. Be sure to follow her Facebook and author pages and join her newsletter for information on upcoming events and giveaways.
Follow the QR codes below:

Connect with Saharra web page

Instagram
@SKSandhu_Author

TikTok
@Saharraksandhuauthor

Made in the USA
Las Vegas, NV
30 September 2023